The Red Dog

Published in the United States by Carole Watterson Troxler
ISBN 13: 978-1544869506
ISBN-10: 1544869509
The Red Dog is printed as a First Edition and made possible by a one-time gift-in-kind offer from Wayne Drumheller, Editor and Founder, The Creative Short Book Writers' Project for book and cover design, content layout and formatting and editing assistance. Second printing, June 28, 2017.
Printing Platform CreateSpace.
Distribution: Amazon.com

The Red Dog

A Tale of the Carolina Frontier

By

Carole Troxler

Locations in *The Red Dog* on a background of Henry Mouzon's 1775 map of the Carolinas. Original at Davidson College.

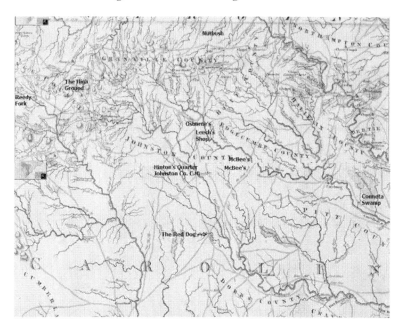

CONTENTS

PREFACE

It is 1764 in the North Carolina Piedmont. Thirteen year-old Lizzy worries for her younger brother. They are orphans, and they have been separated and apprenticed to different masters. In her new location, she faces hard work, a lower social status, and changes in her body that puzzle and confuse her.

As a white girl, Lizzy is curious about slavery, which is not yet secure in the Piedmont. She bonds with ethnically diverse friends, and their help to one another puts them in peril. Throughout, she tries to keep herself steady and make the best of her apprenticeship by thinking about her mother's example. With memories of her mother fading, Lizzy learns to think – and feel – her own way.

While she works in her master's Red Dog Tavern, she learns of grievances that soon will explode in the Regulator Movement. A sequel to *The Red Dog* will find Lizzy with the Regulators during 1769-1771.

Court Day

Lizzy was scared. This was the first time she had been in a court. The people crowding into the log building looked mean. Most were dirty, with matted hair. Where a few clean-looking men sat, their linen hunting shirts brightened the room. Some of them talked quietly, not hollering and honking mucous onto the floor. One or two sitting down close to the table with the little fence around it wore shirts with ruffles. Lizzy could not think why a man would do that, unless it was to make some woman work harder. She doubted the women who did the work were their wives, because they looked rich enough to have some Negro woman — or maybe an old wore-out Negro man -- to do for them. At least, the ruffles gave her something clean to look at. Mother would have called the dandy men "cockscombs," roosters who were crowing with their clothes.

Lizzy caught herself. She was thinking down-mouth thoughts! Mother always told her that thinking down-mouth thoughts would make life ugly. Lizzy hadn't known about life being ugly back when Mother started saying it. She couldn't think what her self-respecting mother would say if she knew why both her children were in this place. No, Lizzy knew what Mother would do, now that she thought on it! So she lifted her head, straightened her back, and glanced sideways at her little brother like she was fully in charge and could stand up for both of them for whatever these old men in the court had in mind. After all, she was 13 years old and not a coward. The hard seat quit paining her buttocks now that she was sitting straight.

Davo was swinging his shoeless feet, too young to feel sheep-like. Lizzy was glad. Davo could be troublesome if he thought people were looking at him sideways, like they wouldn't look straight on him because they were thinking bad about him and wanted to hide their thoughts. Aunt Chassie called this the evil eye, but Lizzy thought the evil eye meant something else. Lizzy reminded herself that she had no call to feel sheep-like because of rabbit skins on Little Brother's feet.

They were clean, except for the road dust on the bottoms. Uncle Frank had showed him how to scrape off the mud so that only dust stayed. Davo's feet sure didn't stink like the woman on the bench down from them, who had taken off a shoe and stretched a misshapen foot. No, Davo's rabbit skins told nothing against her. Or their mother, or poor Papa, drowned those years ago.

She wondered if the sheriff's man who took both pairs of Davo's shoes would be in the court today. She guessed he would, and she added hiding her fear of him to the orders to herself she was lining up in her head. Her brother's feet had outgrown the old pair, but he had hoped to trade them for a horn folding knife. He was growing so fast that the old shoes seemed new, just "broke in good for a new horse," Davo had laughed.

His other shoes were the newest things the man had loaded into the sheriff's wagon, seized by orders from Squire Somebody-or-other as the possessions of their dead mother. The paper the man read out in front of their house said something like "distrain" and "the complaint of" Merchant Pomeroy at Smith's Ferry. He was the young man from Petersburg who had moved here and took over old Mr. Vinson's store, where Mother always traded. Mother always took things to Mr. Vinson whenever she had things to trade throughout the year. Mr. Vinson always wrote in his ledger book how much money the things Mother brought into the store were worth. He wrote down what it was – like five yards of linen thread or three pounds of dried apples – and beside it, the value he would give her for it, so many shillings or pence. The merchant would write all this on one side of his open book, and everything would have the date to it. On the facing page, he wrote everything that Mother bought from the store, along with the date and how much money he charged her for it. Every one of a merchant's customers had two facing pages in the store ledger, with the customer's name across the top. What they took from the store was on the "debit" side, and what they brought into it was on the "credit" side.

Mother took Mr. Vinson dried peaches and apples in late fall and eggs whenever she had extra. But most of her "credit" was from the linen thread and cloth she made. Mother was proud of how good it was. She said it made her feel good to raise her children as well as anybody needed to be raised, and her a widow.

Sometimes Mother bought special things, when she had brought in plenty of goods to trade. Once she bought a book. *Pilgrim's Progress* was its name, and she had read it to Lizzy and Davo before they could read. Lizzy knew the story by heart now. The sheriff's man had taken that too, but he could not take its story about Christian and Christiana out of her head! Anyway, the way the trading between Mother and old Mr. Vinson worked was that at the end of the year, along about Christmas or New Year, Mother went in to settle with him. It was easy to do. He looked up her two facing pages in his store ledger: it had her name in big letters across the top, MRS. O'CANNING. While Mother and Lizzy watched, he added up the credit side and added up the debit side, and there it was, plain as day. One of them owed the other the difference, but usually it was not much.

Sometimes when it happened that Mother had brought in more during the year than she had bought, she settled up with the store by taking something Davo or Lizzy specially wanted. That was how Lizzy got the shiny black ribbons she had looked at every time she came in with Mother. She knew Mother could not make ribbon, because she did not have the special handloom for the narrow fabric. Besides, Mother did not have silkworms or the equipment to make silk thread with the cocoons the worms made. There were people who did all that, and Mr. Vinson got the ribbons and silk cloth from merchants in Wilmington, Cross Creek, Charles Town, or Petersburg. There was never much silk at Vinson's, and it cost more than the linen and wool cloth. Lizzy's silk ribbons were not as thick and shiny as when they were new, but she still had them! If the sheriff's man had known about them, he would have "distrained" them for sure. The ribbons has escaped because Mother had washed and pressed them with the rest of their clothes and had folded the special ribbons in the back of the Bible for next time Lizzy should want them. Mother had thought it strange that a girl Lizzy's age would want black ribbons, rather than pink or celandine. Very sadly, Lizzy now could wear the ribbons in mourning for her mother, which she could not have done with the brighter colors.

The word the sheriff's man had used for everything in the house except a few clothes and Lizzy's own shoes was "chattel." Lizzy had heard the word before but hadn't known what it meant until that awful morning when the man cleared out the house. She remembered the word because it sounded like "cattle." Well, like the word sounded, he took their milch cow too, the two calves, and their hogs and chickens. Everything. All to go to the new merchant Pomeroy at Smith's Ferry. He even took Mother's clothes and shawl, the bed coverlids, and the cloth and yarn Mother was working with when she took sick and died. Lizzy thought and thought about that. It had been only September then; the cloth and yarn would have gone onto Mother's "credit" page rightly. Why didn't Mr. Pomeroy wait until settling-up time?

Here they were, Lizzy with her ribbons strung so tight that the bonnet ruffles nearly hid her face from prying eyes, and Davo swinging his little rabbity feet, waiting for the scary court to decide what would become of them, now that the law made them "orphans of the county." They had no family, home, or way to make trade goods for what they would need.

Suddenly there was less shuffling in the crowd as three men strode to the table at the front of the room and sat together on a bench facing the crowd. It was smoothed down some, and it had a back, unlike the other benches. One of the men was Squire Buchannon, the man who had brought her and Davo here from Aunt Chassie and Uncle Frank's house.

"O-yeh, o-yeh, o-yeh," sang out another man who had walked to the front of the table. He carried a stout pole with something carved at the top, but he did not carry it like a pole. He carried out front, like a big platter. "Honorable court for the

County of Johnston is now in session. All may approach the court as authorized by the law of His Majesty's province of North Carolina promulgated in the Year of Our Lord seventeen and forty-six. All give ear to the honorable Justices Buchannon, Crenshaw, and Hardy presiding." Then he turned the pole straight up and rapped it loudly on the floor, sang out, "God save the king," turned quickly to lay the pole across the front of the table, made a bow, and sat down in the front row. Lizzy would have giggled at his sing-songy speech if she hadn't been so scared. She wondered if he talked that way to his children and all at home.

One of the three justices called out something to the room, and about 15 men lined up in front of the table to speak to them. When each man took his turn, he said something Lizzy could not hear and the justices talked a little, and then Squire Buchannon wrote something down in a ledger book, and the third justice wrote on little pieces of paper and handed them off to men who came over, mostly the ruffled ones. Lizzy wondered how long it would be before they got around to apprenticing orphans.

About Apprentices

On the way to the court this morning, Lizzy had got up her nerve and asked Squire Buchannon what it was all about. She had tried asking Uncle Frank, but he had not wanted to talk about it, and Aunt Chassie just cried when Lizzy asked her. Lizzy didn't think it would bother Squire Buchannon to answer her questions, because Big Boy Todd was driving the carriage, and the squire was free to talk. It was a bright early morning, and she had noticed that grownups sometimes were friendlier then, before they got "wore out by the hackles of the day," as Aunt Chassie would say. Her aunt had wrapped her own coverlid around Lizzy's shoulders against the cold. Inside the carriage, Lizzy pulled Davo under the coverlid with her. They had never been in a carriage before, and its back and sides promised a warmer ride than an open wagon. There even were two bearskins! The squire spread one on the children's combined lap and one on himself.

So Lizzy had asked Squire Buchannon, "Please, Sir, what will happen to my brother and me?"

"You'll be apprenticed out, Child. That means someone will come forward and promise the court that he will teach you a line of work so that you can support yourself when you are grown. He will be the master, and you will be the apprentice. You will work for him, or maybe his wife, and that is how you will learn: by doing what they show you how to do. While you are learning, your master will give you food, clothes, and a place to live."

"Like a Negro slave?"

"Well, no. A slave is a slave for life, and his or her children have to be slaves as well, unless the master takes some unusual action."

"What action?" This was *interesting*. Lizzy had wondered about slaves before and why the only slaves she had seen had been Negroes. Now was her chance to find out.

His answer was quick. "Well, it's too much to talk about now. I was just going to say that you and Little Brother will not be apprentices forever, just for several years. You both should come out of it better off: you'll have a way to make a living, a good recommendation from your master, and a new set of clothes. Plus any tools that are required for the work you have learned. That's the way it's supposed to work. The court's job — my duty as a justice of the peace — is to match you up with people who want apprentices and make sure they keep their word. It's a legal promise they have to make before they can take you."

Lizzy was quiet but then burst out, "but we will go to the same people, won't we? Not me to one place and David to another? Horror made it hard to speak.

"Oh, Child, it would be most unusual if you got the same place. Please do not expect it."

"But David is so little. He always has had me." She was trembling now. Davo was her closest somebody. If either of them ran into trouble, there should be the other to help out. There had to be! Davo was prone to trouble. And the time would come, she knew it, when she would need Davo. She feared for herself as much as for him.

Plainly, the squire did not know what to say. So he said nothing. Neither did Big Boy Todd, who had heard the talking. Todd leaned down his head and rubbed it up and down the back and across the top, mumbling to himself. Lizzy felt a strange comfort from him, even while her trouble sank in, clawing at her insides.

"Do we have to be 'prenticed?" Why can't we just stay on with Aunt Chassie and Uncle Frank? He can teach Davo to farm. We're already helping. Mother showed me how to spin, and we could get a wheel someway, and we could use the yarn for trade like Mother did, along with raising chickens, and eggs, an' . . ."

Squire Buchannon broke her off there, even as she realized that her poor mother's yarn and eggs had been swept away, along with the precious wheel. "It is impossible for you to remain with your uncle and aunt," he said. "They are good people and hard workers, but they have too many mouths to feed even without you two. Yes, Franklin Youngblood is a skilled farmer and in other circumstances could teach David well. You may not know it, but he has no deed for the farm and could lose it without warning. Besides, he is not able to work like he did a few years ago, before the fight at Fort Dobbs tore up his body.

"Zounds!" Davo sprang alive. So he had been listening the whole time, saying nothing! "Uncle Frank fought the Cherokees? He never told me! So that's why he walks crooked and can't bend but so far?"

"And has such trouble sleeping," Lizzy whispered. Poor Uncle Frank. He is ashamed that he can't keep Davo and me fed and clothed, much less give us a start in life. That must be why he would not talk about our going away, and why Aunt Chassie cried so.

Lizzy was calmer now. Strangely, like Todd's head rubbing, knowing that Aunt Chassie and Uncle Frank cared was something Lizzy could hold onto. And whatever fear Davo had picked up from the talk between his sister and the squire was lessened by the news that his own uncle was a hero of the Cherokee War.

Lizzy had been remembering all this while things she did not understand were going on at the justices' table. Suddenly, she heard the word "orphan," and that brought her mind back to the court. The justices gave three children over to a woman and also declared her their guardian. It did not take long. They all had the same last name as the woman, so they must be her kin, Lizzy reckoned. That seemed fair and made Lizzy a little hopeful. But Davo scrunched against her arm, holding still and hard like a rabbit trying to make itself smaller when it sees danger.

They called out Davo's name first: "David O'Canning, son of David O'Canning, to be apprenticed." No sooner had the justice finished the word "apprenticed" before a man called out, "I'll take him." He was one of the dirtiest persons in the room, and Lizzy had noticed him before court started, loudly harking mucous out his nose without using even a rag for a handkerchief. Now she saw the wetness on his sleeve. Her eyes darted to Squire Buchannon, who just for a moment had a surprised frown but quickly straightened his face.

"Leetch," Justice Hardy spoke up, "the boys you had two years ago as 'prentices did not do well. The young one sickened and died, as I recall, and the older boy ran away."

"No fault of mine, Sir, to be sure." Mr. Leetch's face bore a restful smile, but his black eyes darted out from under his bushy eyebrows like beetles running up out of rotten wood. "The young lad was sickly to start on, puking something awful from the start."

"And the one who ran away?" Justice Hardy continued. "Why do you suppose he did that, and did you try to find him?"

"Well, no, I did not advertise to find him. Why pay money to that newspaper in New Bern when I figured he took off the other direction, up the rivers? It was dry then, low water. I did ask on yon side of the Neuse, but he probably made it on across them other rivers, no doubt the Eno and Haw, maybe even over the Yadkin. Besides, he weren't worth going after; rascal kept saying he weren't suited to making wagon wheels."

"Is that what you aim to do with young O'Canning? Make a wheelwright of him?"

"I'm not making just wheels now. I'm making the whole wagons. I'll turn the boy into a proper wagon maker." Leetch tilted his head politely to the magistrates, but he cut his beetle-eyes over to Davo. The boy still was stiff as a board against Lizzy's arm, but he had straightened up and was sitting tall. Lizzy was proud that Davo looked straight at Leetch.

Justice Crenshaw spoke up, the first he had said in Davo's case. "More work to do, Gentlemen. If no objection, let us approve of Rasco Leetch as master for apprentice David O'Canning, due to give bond and take obligation as by law provided," As he spoke, he motioned for Davo and Leetch to come forward.

Davo stood up straight and went forward. Lizzy's heart fell into her stomach. She was glad he did not turn to look at her or say anything but just walked away on his spindly legs and wrapped feet.

The Furred Girl

Lizzy took a deep breath and sat taller. Would she be the next orphan to get a master?

She was not. The justices talked about "deeds" and "proving," and she saw men lay their hand on a Bible and say some words, and then the justice asked them if a signature was a certain person's hand, and they said it was. That was the sort of thing they had done while her mind had wandered back to the ride to court and her talk with Squire Buchannon. Would they get back to orphan matters, or was Davo the only orphan they intended to give out today?

No, orphan-time was not over. Squire Hardy called out again, "Disposition of orphans and base-born children. Come forward, Phoebe Hawkins and Elke Tikell, with your infants."

Two young women, each carrying a baby, walked to the desk. One baby was older than the other, and he had dark skin and hair.

Justice Crenshaw called out over the crowd, "Phoebe Hawkins, having stated under oath that Josiah Kime had got her with the infant in her arms, and the last court having ordered Josiah Kime to appear at this court, the court inquires if the same Josiah Kime be present, as required, in this court?" There was no answer.

Crenshaw looked at a man on the front bench and raised his eyebrows. "Constable?" The man replied, "Sir, Josiah Kime could not be found in his neighborhood of Mickey's Creek or settlements thereabouts. It was told to me that he has gone into Virginny."

Again, Crenshaw spoke quickly, "The purported father not being present to be fined, Phoebe Hawkins is to be taken to the public whipping post and receive 20 lashes. Next case, Elke Tikell," and he peered down at the boy in her arms.

"Did you, Elke Tikell, give birth to this mulatto child?"

"Yes, Sir. He is mine." Her voice was light and wavery. The baby chewed on his fist and bumped his head against her shoulder.

The justice looked out among the crowd and cleared his throat.

"A white woman not being allowed to keep her mulatto child, a master is required to provide food, housing and safety for the child until he is of serviceable age and then to take him as apprentice. The child is freeborn and cannot be sold. It is good to bring up such a child in a household where there are Negroes, and in particular where there is some Negro woman to have the care and raising of him, amongst her other duties. Who comes forward for this child?"

There was a pause and some shuffling in the room, during which Elke Tikell spoke up, louder than before, "His name is Bentjamin."

Surprised, Crenshaw darted a look at her, just as a woman rose and said, "I can take charge of the child." Her brown woolen skirt and bodice looked new, and a tan shawl that was worn but spotless topped the bodice and her creamy shift. The crowd quietened as she spoke.

"Widow McBee," Crenshaw gasped, and then smiled, "Please come forward." he motioned to Elke Tikell without looking at her, "Come on over here, Gal." But Elke was already on her way, with a surprised and almost happy look on her face. The justices spoke in low, quick voices and then the two women leaned over the table and wrote on the paper Crenshaw put before them. He told Mrs. McBee to put her hand on the Bible and say something he told her; then when he motioned his head at the mother of Benjamin Tikell, she stood close to the older woman and handed her the child. Mrs. McBee touched Elke's arm as she motioned for her to walk in front. They turned from the bench, all eyes fastened on them heading toward the door. When they passed the bench where the older woman had sat, a middle-aged Negro woman rose to follow them toward the door.

While Lizzy watched, trying to take in what had happened, she heard Crenshaw call sharp and fast, "Case of Elizabeth O'Canning, age 13, orphan of David O'Canning, for apprenticeship." He looked around the room and continued, "Bring the child forward." There was no one to "bring" her "forward," but Lizzy guessed she was supposed to come to the table in front of the justices, so she started there. Just then, Squire Buchannon nodded to her and smiled, so she felt a little easier. But the silence was strange.

She felt people looking at her. She knew she was dressed decently, in her warm linsey-woolsey skirt, still reddish brown from when she and Mother had dyed the batches of linen and wool yarn about two years ago. Mother had strung the woolen thread long ways onto the loom first and then woven the linen thread across it. She saved this piece when she took other cloth to the merchant for trade. The skirt was one of the last things Mother had made before she sickened, and Lizzy had worn it little. It was about the only nice thing the sheriff's men had left. The linen blouse Lizzy wore had been Mother's. Aunt Chassie had taken the blouse after Mother died, and then she gave it to Lizzy after the sheriff's men came and went. It was creamy white like the Widow McBee's, but Lizzy was still a frail girl and did not think of cutting a figure like that lady for a long time yet. She liked the house-bonnet she was wearing, and maybe it helped her hold her head high while people stared. The bonnet had escaped the sheriff's raid only because Lizzy had it on her head when the men came! The caul part of it puffed in full gathers over her wrapped hair. Lizzy had a lot of long hair. She had braided it today, but the gathers let the fullness show. Around her face, only bits of hair peeked under the ruffled brim. Her hair was not yellow like Davo's, but it seemed close kin to the linen she loved. At last, she reached the table where the magistrates were.

More silence! Well, almost silence. She could hear whispers and then they got louder, but no one was speaking up to take her as an apprentice. Then she heard a squeaky voice louder than the others, coming from the back of the room and then moving through the crowd toward her, on short, slightly bowed legs:

"If it please your worships, I'll tek the gull. I, Tomm Toliver and my good wife, we'll train her up to the business of taverning at our public house, the Red Dog, licensed last term by yer good selves. Only, I . . . ." and by this time, he was talking head-to-head with the justices. Lizzy could not hear them. Squire Buchannon seemed to be asking the man questions, and the man seemed to be answering. The squire cleared his throat and called out, "This court will observe noon interval until two o'clock."

People got up noisily and started leaving the room. Lizzy did not know what to think. Squire Buchannon stood beside her. "It's all right, Child, Mr. Toliver did not come to court expecting to take an apprentice, and he has not the money for the bond. Between now and two o'clock, he will try to get men to sign with him to guarantee his bond, and if he does, he will be your master."

"Please, Squire," she interrupted, "does this mean the man is buying me?"

"Oh, no. The 'bond' is the amount of money he would have to pay the court if he should fail to train you and give you a set of clothes at the end of your five years' service. I don't know Toliver well. He's a new man in Johnston County, just opened a public house down near Dobbs County. I don't expect it to be a bad place for you." Buchannon looked away a bit, then leaned closer to Lizzy and said, "I expect much will depend on how well you get along with Toliver's wife." He smiled and walked away.

Outside, Lizzy circled the courthouse, looking for Davo and the wagon maker Mr. Leetch who had taken him. They must have left after Leetch got what he came for, she guessed. She found a big rock some ways from the crowd, where she could think and watch people. She had seen so much, but the big question of her own self, Lizzy O'Canning, Orphan-To-Be-Given-Out, made her so numb that she did not cringe from the January cold.

All along the flat road that went by the small courthouse, Lizzy could see people hallooing to one another, trading all sorts of things and arguing about the trades. Some big boys and girls were walking in pairs, around and around the building. A man-boy ran up to one of the couples and said something to the boy, and first thing Lizzy knew, people were circling around them, cheering and jeering a fistfight. The girl ran, but other girls enjoyed the fight. One of them left the circle and walked toward Lizzy.

Lizzy's first thought was to be a little afraid of her. She was older than Lizzy, with straight brown hair that fell loose on her shoulders beneath a floppy deerskin hat tied under her chin. Her hair was the colors of a buckeye: streaks on top were tan, like the eye of a buckeye, and those streaks looked worn and frazzled, but the underneath hair was dark and shiny. She wore animal skins near about all over. They looked to be nicely tanned and well fitted to her body but so grimy that Lizzy thought the girl must be wearing them night and day all winter. The only cloth showing was strips of wool wrapped around her lower legs and tied down with strips of leather. For shoes, she wore different kinds of skins, some with fur. They seemed to be expertly tied or laced together, not flimsy like Davo's makeshift rabbit skins. For all her surprising appearance, there was nothing that looked makeshift about this girl. She walked like she knew where she was going and what she would do when she got there. Lizzy wished she could be like that!

"Well, now, here's the girl that might go to the Red Dog. I hope Tomm Toliver finds enough bond to get you for a 'prentice." She grinned sideways, "Seeing as nobody else spoke up to take you home to their wives. That's who you'll really work for, you know: Goody Toliver." Lizzy just looked while the girl rattled on, "Most of the girls who get 'prenticed are set to housework so they turn out knowing how to be good servants or good wives." She tossed her head and added, "About the same thing."

"Are they never taught anything else," Lizzy asked, "like yarn and cloth work, or sewing?"

"Not here they're not. They just do all the general things women do. At the Red Dog, there'll be cooking and cleaning enough to keep a girl busy without getting into fancy work."

Lizzy was sheep-faced for not knowing, but she asked, "Just what *is* the Red Dog? Is a public house like a tavern – a place where people sit down and buy something to eat and drink and pay to spend the night?"

"Sure, you got the notion of it. It's mostly for people going from one place to another that don't camp and cook their food and sleep out. They can pay to have their horses fed and stabled, too."

"Is that a public house on yon side of the courthouse?" Lizzy asked. I've watched folks going in and out, and I could see big tables."

"Sure is," the furred girl agreed. "Loudest place in Hinton's Quarter for sure. My brothers are getting their victuals in there now. They won't let me go with them. But I brought a big old sweet 'tato from home. Eat some with me. I got enough."

"Zounds, thanks. I have got hungry." Both girls were sitting on the rock now. The sweet potato was still warmish, and it was moist with bear grease. Lizzy was used to butter, but she knew plenty of folks used bear grease.

Just then, a wagon rumbled toward them, with two dogs yapping at the heels of the horses. The driver, a smart-looking black man wearing a red and black plaid vest under his coat, struck at them with his whip, his eyes straight ahead. After the dogs whimpered away, the girls recognized the women in the wagon.

"Look, there go the Widow McBee and her Negro Minerva, with the mulatto baby they got."

Lizzy was amazed. "How do you know her servant's name? Do you know Mrs. McBee?"

"Oh, everybody knows them. Minerva has spirit powers. Bad people are scared of her, and they ought to be. She can tell you where lost things are, and that's not all. She can tell where stolen things are hidden, and *who stole them.* That's her husband driving the wagon. My brothers say Gaspar McBee's the best man for training horses in this country. Widow McBee buys young horses and raises colts from them, and Gaspar trains them. People come here from way up in Virginny and Pennsylvany to buy her horses.

"So. Maybe that baby will be looked after all right, even without his mamma?"

"Ho, I tell you, that baby is a lucky little ducky to have Minerva to raise him. A far sight better than any base-born child I know, white, black, mulatto, Suponi, Tuskarories, or anything else between." She spoke in a lower voice, "you saw how Widow McBee brought the baby's mamma along with them out of the court? I saw them talking a long time, friendly-like. They'll have to be careful, but I'm thinking the Widow McBee might make sure that baby knows who his mamma is as he grows up. If she takes her mind to it, she'll do it."

"How did Mrs. McBee get to be so, so – free? Like she owns herself. Is it because she's rich?"

"She wasn't so rich a while back. Her husband cut a fine figure, but everybody allows how she's made the money since he's been dead. There's talk that he was a free spender. She's a good liv-ver, but she don't throw money around."

That didn't quite answer Lizzy's question, so she just asked, "How did Mr. McBee die?"

"Colonel McBee got himself killed at Fort Dobbs. He led the men that marched from these parts, and the ones that came back allowed as how he had been the bravest man in the fight. Oh, they do still go on about Colonel McBee."

Lizzy thought the furred girl might be the smartest person she ever met who was not a grownup. Now she had a really hard question from the morning's court, so she burst out:

"Those two women with babies the court called 'baseborn' – that means the women were not married, right?" Before the girl finished nodding, Lizzy kept talking, "But why weren't they treated the same? One is to be lashed-whipped but gets to keep her baby, and the other had to give over her baby! Can you tell me the difference?"

The girl frowned, not at Lizzy but at the ground, her jagged hair falling forward. "I don't know what's at the bottom of Elke Tikell having to give up her baby on account of its having a black daddy, but I know it's got something to do with making free Negroes be more like slaves than like white people." The girl spoke slowly. "Babies are born free if their mammas are free, whatever color the mammas are, and they are born slaves if their mammas are slaves, no matter how light. What color their daddies are, and if their daddies are free or slave, they don't make no difference about the baby being free or not. That much I have had explained to me. There's got to be lot more to it, though." Then she looked up at Lizzy.

"So, Elke had to give up her baby because it was part Negro, but Phoebe's baby was all white, and she got to keep it. What was it about the man Phoebe said was the daddy?"

Now the girl was on firmer ground about explaining. "Well, Phoebe will be lash-whipped for having a baby without being married. Sometimes they lash-whip the daddy too. But what the

JPs really want from the daddy is for him to give a bond promising to give so much money a year to help pay for the baby's food and all. The daddy of Phoebe's baby is long-gone from here, run off. He was supposed to show up in court today to make his bond.

"You're going too fast. What's a JP?"

"Oh, you know, justice of the peace, those men that sat at the table at the front of the court and ran the court."

"Oh, you mean the squires, the magistrates, like Squire Buchannon that brought me here today?"

Sure, like Squire Buchannon. The justices of the peace are the main men that run things around here. They say how much taxes folks have to pay, and they set other men to working on the roads. And they decide things in the law courts, like today."

Satisfied about what JP meant, Lizzy got back to the babies. "Why was the white daddy supposed to take a bond but the black daddy was not?"

It's about not spending tax money. The court turned the baby with the Negro daddy over to Widow McBee, so the county won't have any expense in raising it. But the white baby – it's staying with its mamma, and she might run up on hard times. She's got no land, or animals, or tools, or anything else to turn a coin on. If she can get work somebody will pay her for, and if she can keep the work, well and good. But if she runs out of any way to feed the baby, maybe even gets sick and down herself, and if she's got no family to help her out, then the county court will pay somebody to give her and the baby some food. That's called "poor relief," and it's in the law. That's what the JPs are afeared of, having to pay poor relief for babies without daddies."

The girl seemed proud that she could tell Lizzy so much, and she chattered on. "There's two ways babies don't have daddies. If the daddy dies, or if he's not married to the mother. The court can't do anything about married daddies dying, but they can try to make the daddies that are not married take a bond to help keep the babies fed and all. See?"

It was a lot to hold in Lizzy's head, but it was *interesting,* and Lizzy reckoned she would think about it some later. What puzzled her now was how this unusual girl knew so much about important things. So Lizzy stood up, put her right hand out to shake the girl's hand, and made a little speech:

"My name is Lizzy O'Canning. I am pleased to make your acquaintance. I want to know your name, and I want you to tell me how it is that you know so much."

The girl made a face but quickly grinned. She stood, looked Lizzy straight in the eye, and shook her hand. Lizzy was surprised that the girl was no taller than Lizzy herself.

"And I am Ruly Morgin. I am a person who listens. And I watch. I have no schooling, but my Pa and my brothers say I'm canny. I like to see and hear things in court, at dances, at preachings, and wherever else people mingle. My brothers almost always come to court for the trading outside. I like to decide whether I think people are telling lies. I myself try to tell the truth, unless it's extry troublesome."

The court continued at two o'clock, and Lizzy was apprenticed to Tomm Toliver three minutes later. They left the court quickly. Ruly Morgin gave Lizzy a calm nod, and Lizzy breathed in deep and pictured the Widow McBee.

Tomm Toliver

They were silent while they walked to Toliver's wagon. He motioned for her to sit beside him. As he took up the reins, he glanced at her and muttered, "'Twill be a good place for ye, Gull; ye'll soon see. Reach underneath and use the blanket."

"Thank you. Please, Sir, do you know where Mr. Leetch lives, who has taken my little brother?"

"He's said to move about a bit. Last I heered, he was up on the other side of the Neuse, near about to Big Jeff Osborne's place. The wagon maker who used to be at Osborne's moved on to Rowan. Reckon Leetch can do well enough to stay in the place. If he keeps steady with his work, I mean."

"Will there be any time I can go to see him or to see my aunt and uncle?"

"Hold on, now, don't get ahead. We'll have to see about that in time to come. Ye'ill be a good ways off from Frank Youngblood. What kin are ye?"

"Mrs. Chastity Youngblood is my mother's sister."

"Yes, her with her high-flown ways, there's no surprise. Any other kin ye know about?"

Lizzy was pleased that he was interested in her family. She did not know yet that he was asking because he wanted to know where she might be likely to run off to.

"I have some people on Deep River, but I hardly know them. They're my mother's and my father's people."

"Well, Gull," Toliver reared back in the seat, making it move behind Lizzy, "Yer home for the next five years will be with Tomm and Goody Toliver. There'll be food, a place to sleep, and plenty of work to keep ye from pining on yer miseries. And to be certain ye know, I inform ye now that runaway apprentices get caught, just like runaway Negroes do, and they be brought back to punishment. It would not please me to see the lash on yer back, but that be what would happen." He turned toward her to be sure she understood.

Both remained silent for a while, Lizzy getting more and more distressed. She tried to recall her mother's warning about down-mouth thoughts, but nothing good came to mind to think about. They came to a place where the road changed, and Toliver turned the wagon a sharp right, onto a route that was less of a road than they had travelled from Hinton's Quarter.

Toliver, feeling a little sorry for the girl, started talking again.

"No need to be in the dark about where ye are, Gull. If we had stayed straight on the flat road, we would have got to the ferry that crosses the Neuse. But my place be on this side of the river. We'll go south for a good spell on this new-cut road and cross some waters to get to my place."

Lizzy wondered how long it would take. The sun was past its warmest angle, and this talk about crossing "some waters" made her wonder if they would have to camp for the night. She was afraid to ask, and it wouldn't change the answer if she did, so she held her tongue.

"Yas, the new road brings more people to our ford. The way down from the Roanoke to the Pee Dee has been here before any of us were. Old Barnwell used it when he came up from South Car'liny to fight the Tuskarories. They call it the Green Path, and it crosses the creek where we live. But the new-cut road, the one we're on now, well it crosses the Green Path right about our ford. Travelling folks is tired, hungry and thirsty, and their horses be about wore-out from dragging across creeks to get that far. Yas, once we're there, Gull, ye'ill see what a good eye for turning the coins old Tomm has – not leaving aside his Good Wife, of course."

The "new-cut road" was no more than a series of blazed cuts on trees with some rocks laid in the lowest places. Lizzy was afraid the wagon would break up in some of the bad spots. Now she understood why Toliver's wagon was so narrow. It was better suited to such a "road" than the full-sized wagon that could use the road they had taken from Hinton's Quarter where the courthouse was.

"How new is this road, Mr. Toliver?"

"Oh, now, less than year old, 'tis." He rushed his words, explaining, "I was part o' the road crew what cut it out, I was. Got up a petition, soonz I moved to the place. Course, I couldn't a got the petition signed and all nor got the court to order a road cut by myself. Old Squire Needham favored me with wording up the petition and signing his own name first. Left it open in my public house for any man to sign. No, they'd not a' signed it without the squire's name. The fellows about here didn't know me yet, ye see, I just came into these parts. I dare say they would pay me mind now, how-some-ever."

Lizzy didn't understand much of what he meant.

"You worked on the road. You knew it would bring folks to your tavern. But who else helped cut the road, and why did they want to?"

Old Tomm laughed. "Don't know as they wanted to help, but they had to! The county court ordered all the able men in this district to turn out for road work on the certain days. Ever' man owes two weeks in a year to keep up the roads. Young Squire Needham — he's the old squire's son — he was the boss over that road-cutting, and of course the road was put through their land."

"But some of the road crew did not have land on the road?"

"Yas, that's right. Some didn't, so ye might say they were working for the other fellows." Was it Lizzy's imagination, or did Toliver look sheep-like? Then, "Court made some road orders this morning. Did ye not hear them?"

"No, Sir, I wasn't paying good attention." Now Lizzy was the sheep-like one. She liked hearing him talk, though.

"Do many more people come to the Red Dog now that there are two roads going there?"

Her words pleased Toliver.

"Oh, now, so ye knows the name o' my tavern, does ye? Clever gull. Why, yes, there's enough folks coming that my Goody needs help with the warshing and cooking and all. Ever since the road opened, she's been saying she wanted a gull. I forgot that orphans were put out to masters in January in this colony, me still being new. Took me by surprise this morning. Goody'll be pleased." Then he added, "But she'll not let on none, for certain." Lizzy wondered if Mrs. Toliver's real name was "Goody." She had heard people address married women as "Good Wife" So-and-So or "Goody" if they knew them, but is "Goody" anyone's real name? She didn't think she would ask. Instead, she looked at Toliver and said,

"Sir, is there really a red dog in your public house?"

Again, he laughed, not in a hurtful way, but like he enjoyed the question. "There be a red dog, but he's only a picture painted on a board." Lizzy looked puzzled, so he went on:

"I could have called the place 'Toliver's' like most do here in Car'liny, but I harkened back to the style of Ireland, where we came from, and to England. Why, some towns and villages there have so many public houses they all have signs for travelers to know them by. And same as here, most folk don't have their letters, so they look for a picture hanging over the building, like 'the sign of the Golden Lion,' or 'the Laughing Mermaid,' or 'the Red Dog,' don't ye see?"

It was Lizzy's turn to be pleased. She wanted to keep him talking, because it helped her not be scared when the wagon twisted and bumped. She was about to ask more when the hill they went down veered toward a creek, one of the "waters" Toliver had talked about.

"Here we are, Gull, at the ford on Crabtree Creek. I reckon it be low enough to stay in the wagon, and Snap can foot it across. If we get in trouble, we can go back and cross higher."

Lizzy knew that in summer people would just get out of a wagon and get across a stream any way they could, but that was unthinkable in this cold. Toliver got out at the water's edge, stroked the horse's flank, and spoke encouraging sounds. Lizzy grabbed up the bottom of the blanket and pulled it and her legs up, expecting the wagon floor to drag beneath the water.

In they went, Toliver back behind the reins and leaning forward, half-standing, and Lizzy with her feet drawn up into the seat. Snap's ears flared back, and he did a fine prance through the water —until his right side dipped, like his foot had gone in a hole, and he started to rear up. Clearly, the horse had been in places like this before, and he caught himself short of a full rear-up. Lizzy was so thankful. If Snap had kept on rearing, they would have tumbled into Crabtree Creek for certain.

Toliver was struggling to guide the scared horse. After testing another spot for Snap's footing and seeing the same effect, Toliver began urging the horse back to the first bank. Snap seemed glad and jostled them up the bank. Toliver's face was pale when he tried to laugh,

"Mother Crabtree does not want us on her lap today. We will try her shoulder." He soon found ground alongside the creek for the wagon to trudge upstream, and they crossed without more excitement. Still, they had to find a way back to the road. Snap sensed the way as much as Toliver did. Settled back into the roadway, Lizzy surprised herself by thinking the crossing had been a kind of fun. But wait, the next creek might be deeper, because they were following the river downstream. She didn't want to ask how many waters lay ahead, but she really would like to know.

"Do you think my little brother will have got to Mr. Leetch's yet? They left Hinton's Quarter around noon, I think." She hoped her questioning would not annoy Toliver, but he smiled,

"More than likely they are safe there already. The road up there's better than this."

Lizzy hoped Davo had supper and a place to sleep and was warm. She wanted to think there was a kind person there. Davo was brave, but this was hard. "Is Mr. Leetch married? — or do you know?" She added, after Toliver did not answer right away.

"I can't say as I know, Gull, I just can't say as I know." He spoke more slowly than Lizzy liked.

"You came from Ireland. Tell me about it please, and did Mrs. Toliver come from there?" Lizzy knew it would not help to keep thinking on Davo.

"I were but a lad when we left: my parents, two sisters, and me. We stopped in Brunswick County in Virginny, and my father worked for a man with a grand piece o' land in tobac and corn. My ma warshed for the family, my two sisters went as servants to a new settlement, and I helped Father farm for the man. Our people were used to working for landlords back in County Wicklow. Back there, I would have done it all my life. I was a fast learner in the growing of Old To-bac. I made me some money once I got the landlord to share the crop with me instead of giving me wages. Father thought I was mad, giving up steady wages, and I do confirm that it was a gamble, one such as only a young one would take. If the crops had failed, I would 'a been ruint."

"But they didn't fail, did they?" Lizzy liked to listen to Tomm Toliver, and Tomm liked to listen to himself.

"I had a run of luck with three years o' good crops and good prices. I went in wit' some other young fellows, and we wagoned crops to Norfolk. The Hamilton merchant house sent my tobac to Glasgow and sent me back to Brunswick County with their credit notes as good as gold. I never took any cash but did take a few supplies and some goods to trade back home."

"How long did you work for the landlord?"

"Only the three crops, Gull. With my trade goods, I peddled awhile, looking over the country to buy me some land. When I found It, I got Hamilton to change my notes over to the man who sold it. I had enough left to fix up a house and set up farming. By that time, I was in a mind to marry, and Goody was handy and in the mind too, so there we were. Stayed there ten year, we did. Happy times, some of them." His voice trailed off.

"But not all of them happy, Sir?"

"'Twas the babes. All four died before they were two year."

"I feel for your sorrow, surely I do."

"Say nothing of this to my wife, mind ye. After a time she gave up, and she don't cotton to babes. 'Twas her feelings that first put me in mind to keep a house for the public. Farming was wearing on both of us, with no chil'ren to help. We had life enough in us to start out something new and in a new place. Ain't that what these colonies are about? It took me a while to sell out, but prices on land in that part of Virginny were going up fast. A heap of folks had moved there when we did. Chil'ren growing up there needed land, more land than there was. I waited for the right money to come along, while I kept clearing more land and putting up more fences, ready for a buyer."

"So that's when you moved here? When you sold your land?"

"I knew some men who travelled back and forth through North Car'liny, and they acquainted me with the land business here. Enough to know where a man could get good title and where he couldn't. Fellow that owned the place I bought, he had a bad run o' luck, being down and sick for a while — he let the place run down, couldn't help it, I reckon. His neglect made his price lower. To top off his luck, his wife died, and he had nobody to do her work. Already in debt, he couldn't afford

Negro help or even a white servant, so he was ready to sell out when I turned up and made an offer."

Lizzy thought it sounded easier than it likely was, and she hoped she would hear Mrs. Toliver's account of these changes someday. The girl judged Toliver to be canny about money and tucked that away in her mind. Plainly, making money was high up on his list of Important Things.

"Sir, I hope that I can be of good use to you in your business these five years. I expect you and your wife can teach me some useful things about managing a public house. I have reason to help you make a success with your new start." Right off, Lizzy feared she had said too much. She meant the words, but maybe they sounded too important for an apprentice girl to say.

Toliver seemed to think so and was wary.

"Ye'll not be learning to manage, but to clean, warsh, and cook as my wife tells ye. She will be, I warn ye, a strong taskmistress, and ye are to obey her in every detail. To do so be the only way to secure yer contentment." He added, "and mine."

Light was nearly gone when Lizzy saw the next big stream, too late to cross before day.

"We will camp here, in a low place in case a night wind rises."

Lizzy moved quietly from the wagon, glad to be on her feet again. Looking about in the dusk, she found dry limbs and brush and quickly moved them to the low place where she thought Toliver would want a fire. She was the servant now, not a guest.

Toliver seemed pleased, and his fire gave them more light. Lizzy asked if she could untie Snap from the wagon, and she led him to a spot where he could drink without danger of miring. Toliver told her where the oats and feedbag were, and Lizzy felt some kinship and gratitude toward the animal as she fed him.

She watched as Toliver stirred creek water into the ground-up parched corn from his bag. His iron skillet was heating in the fire, and grease from earlier use made it shiny and ready for the mush. Lizzy was hungry and too tired to worry about what

31

would happen to her and Davo. She slept under the blanket, her feet near the fire.

A Surprise for Miz Goody

She woke to the smell of the same food cooking again. This time, there were tea leaves steeping in two metal cups, each fitted into a wooden bottom for holding, and she drank hers greedily.

"Surprised to have proper tea out here, are ye, Gull? Well, no reason a good tavern-keeper can't carry some of 'is goods wi' 'im."

Feeling good after the tea and mush, she was brave enough to ask how many more waters they had to cross after the rushing one before them. "Oh, nothing terrible. A little 'un or two, then we'll be at the Red Dog. It's on 'is side of the next big creek. Now, 'is one right here bears thinking on. We might ought to waggle upstream, like we did yestiddy, and not venture an upset, not this close to home. You bring Snap on to the wagon. I'll harness 'im up while you place 'ese goods in 'e wagon; you recall how I had 'em packed, now?"

Lizzy was glad she did, and they started meandering along the creek to a more shallow crossing.

"What is this creek, Sir?" She felt a need to know where she was in these strange parts.

"It's Swift Creek. Right name, ain't it be? I been told 'ey named this creek before any others around it, on account of how it runs. It gets tamer up beyond the fork, where they call it Walnut Creek or Walnut Tree Creek. Hard to come up wi' names for all 'e creeks, but 'at's how to know yer whereabouts. You did right in asking, Gull." After some hard time getting the wagon through the undergrowth, Toliver declared that they'd better go on past the fork and cross both streams instead of one rushing one.

It did not take long for Lizzy to feel tired, and she knew Snap was tired already too, and nervous, by the time the wagon got across the second stream and they headed back toward the new-cut road. What would they do if they could not find any trees with the marks cut to show the way? She guessed Toliver would know which way to go, or at least Snap would. Lizzy herself was not much traveled. She would have to pay attention. Ruly likely could read the woods and know how to get about. She wished she could see a blazed tree before Mr. Toliver did, so he would think she was smart and be glad he took her. She sat tall and looked hard, just like he did. It was not a time for talking. She noticed they kept in sight of the creek. It twisted and turned something fierce, but sooner or later, it would have to get back to the road. Thinking this, Lizzy realized that they had to be sure they kept going downstream, not get turned around with the creek's twists and start going upstream! That would be away from the road.

Toliver whooped when he saw the first blaze and then quickly found another to point the way. Lizzy had not seen either of them at first, so she asked how he knew where to look for the cut marks.

"Only trick I know about it is to remember a man cut the blaze wi' a blade he could swing while he rode along on a horse. So you look about that high up 'e trees. Keep watching as we go along; ye'ill get used to picking 'em out."

It was along in the afternoon when they got to Toliver's. It had been clouding up most of the day, and they entered a low fog as they came in view of buildings of different sizes, scattered helter-skelter down the hill toward the creek. Sure enough, she saw a flat wooden sign fastened to a tree, with a red dog painted on it. Lizzy could not tell which building was the house, or if the house was a different building from the tavern, or what the sheds were. She knew public houses had some place, a stable or barn of some sort, to shelter horses. Maybe some of these gray log buildings were for animals.

As she looked at a low building with sturdy doors at both ends, she saw a Negro boy come out of it and run toward them. "Mr. Tomm, you're sure home! Mrs. Goody 'bout to send me to the squire to raise the hue-cry on your account." He quit speaking when he saw the girl and moved to Toliver's side of the wagon.

"Snap pulled us home again, Cicero. Miss Lizzy, this is my boy in charge of the stable and horses, and anyt'ing else we set him to do. Cicero, Miss Lizzy is to be helper to my wife, and with my wife's permission she may likewise call upon yer help."

Lizzy thought Toliver's speech to the boy was strangely formal. She thought she understood that he was telling the Negro he must call her "Miss Lizzy" and obey her.

The wagon had reached a large circle between the two most important-looking buildings. The smaller one looked very old, and the other was new and in the process of getting larger. It was like a jumble of boxes fastened together, some old and others quite new. The largest and newest "box" had two levels and big rock chimneys on opposite sides. What Lizzy was anxious to see was Mrs. Goody Toliver. Lizzy had tried not to imagine how the woman who would control her life for five years would be, but in truth, she feared her already.

If Lizzy had let her imagination run wild, she could not have dreamed up the person who stepped out of the smaller house. She was weirdly pretty. Small but fleshy, particularly at the low neck of her shift, where she wore NO KERCHIEF. The bodice below her bosom was laced tight, and her waist was small. The skirt flaring out below the waist suggested there was ample flesh at her hips. The main thing, though, was the woman had different colors of skin, and most of what Lizzy could see looked like a pale lizard with spots. Plainly, the woman had spent much time in the sun without a bonnet or long sleeves. Her arms below the elbows had bigger dark splotches than the freckles on her face and bosom. There was some kind of stain on her lips and cheeks and the tops of her breasts, like berry juice, but there were no berries this time of year. The reddish hair poking out from her house cap looked like it might be streaked, like Ruly's.

Lizzy saw all this while Mrs. Toliver's eyes poked out at her, like yellow-brown mushrooms. After that, all Lizzy could notice was the screeching.

"What be this possum-faced creatur ye've brought along home?"

"Goody Love, Goody Love," Toliver was saying already, "This be the very sarvant gull ye've been needing."

"Sarvant? Wrong color! I wanted a proper sarvant, not some flighty miss what'll leave rather than work! Duraman! Idjit, Idjit, why can ye not get it right?"

"She can't leave, Goody Love, she's bound to us as orphan apprentice!" Tomm had to say this four times before Goody could hear above her own noise. Then she got louder:

"Then we'll have not'ing for her after her time! W' a black gull we could've kept the boy from going off the place, and we'd have young 'uns to sell. D'ye not see the way the world's going, Tomm Toliver! It will get to where people will have to have Negros jest to hold their own, let alone make more money. Orphan apprentice, my arse! Idjit! She'll not be worth what she gobs down in five years.

Now Tomm hollered back, "Listen to me, 'oman, the gull be healthy and a good learner. She can help us build up 'is place. Ye can put her to warshing and scrubbing as good as any black gull can, to keep bedclothes for 'em new rooms we're just afore having. More travelers be coming by already, lak we knew the ey would w' the new-cut road. 'Sides, Lizzy has mannerly ways and talks well. She'll make this a bright spot on 'eir travels."

At that, Goody climbed a higher rung on her ladder of rage, and Tomm instantly knew he had put his mouth in a bad spot.

"Oh, Lizzy, is it? So she's a lizard and not a possum? A bright spot?? Make this a bright spot??"

"Not as much as you brighten it, Goody Love, but one more candle – smaller and weaker—to cheer all who stop at the sign of the Red Dog."

Lizzy had shrunk back from them when Tomm started hollering. She did not listen as they kept railing. She instinctively walked toward the only other person there, Cicero, but huddled into herself.

"You scared, Missy, you scared." It was not a question.

"Do they go on like this a lot?"

"They do, but after Mr. Tomm say his piece, he let Mrs. Goody wear herself out, and all be over."

He sounded sure, so Lizzy asked, "How long have you been with them?"

"Two summers and three winters. Mr. Tomm got me in Pennsylvany. He goes there to trade, time to time."

"Did you always live in Pennsylvania?

"One summer and winter in Pennsylvany. I worked for an Irishman, like Mr. Tomm. That's where I learned horse and cow work, and to talk like that man. I raised a crop there, but I already knew how to crop. My Ma trained me, before all us was taken."

"Enough of yer wasting time over there. Come along, ye!" Goody kept her angry voice but looked calmer. Lizzy rushed to join her stride toward a building set off by itself. Cicero took the horses and wagon to one of the barns.

"Here be the kitchen, where some of ye work will be, and ye'ill sleep."

Lizzy quickly caught on that this was where Goody cooked, and the food had to be carried to the main buildings. She was glad to see a path of short logs, split in half longwise then placed crosswise next to one another and with their flat sides turned up to walk on. Lizzy reckoned she would be carrying food, and she could go between the buildings without miring up in mud. She had noticed other such paths as this between some of the buildings, all looking new.

"Ma'am, I believe you and Mr. Toliver have made the Red Dog larger?" she asked carefully. Where do your travelers eat and sleep?"

"Well, not in the kitchen, if ye be worrit," the woman snapped. "Aye," her tone brightened, "We are after making the sheds secure and building us a Manor House. We already sleep on the second story our own sels, and 'twill be more beds on the first floor. And a parler," she added with a lift of her head.

"The older building next the Manor House," Lizzy continued, "is that the public house itself, where visitors eat and sleep?"

"Aye, 'tis. The old Red Dog as we found it. There still be a picher of 'im over the fire-board. We 'spect ordinary folk to sleep in the old building and quality ones to stay in the Manor House. 'Course, we'll be charging 'em more. We may come to be carrying trays of food to the Manor House, when times git busy, don't ya know?" Goody was almost pleasant as she envisioned the fruits of expansion.

"What shall I do first?" A pot of dried green beans, already soaked and seasoned and well along in cooking, made the kitchen smell good. Lizzy wanted to start on the right foot.

"There be 'taties down the root cellar to have with 'em leather britches yer smelling. Bring up enough to feed ten, and put 'em over the fire for stewing."

Lizzy was about to ask if she should save the peelings when Goody barked, "Do rub the skins good and clean with corncobs and water and save 'em back for making bread." Lizzy knew how to cover the clean skins with water and set them by to catch yeast from the air, but she did wonder how Goody made enough bread for the public. Besides, Mother caught yeast only in summer.

Once she got the potatoes up and was cleaning them, she asked how long it took to get yeast in cold weather. Goody scorned the question: "I jest use the peels to mash up with what's left of the 'taties. I use beer for more yeast in winter. I'll show ye tonight, and bread making 'twill be yer job after that." Ye'll be here handy-like for getting up early to start it. Then you can milk cows after starting the bread."

"Somebody will have to show me how to milk cows."

"Mercy! A gull not a milker! I might be a-knowing it! No mind. Cicero knows cows and can show ye, and I'll make sure ye pour it up cleanly and all. Must be careful with milk and such, powerful careful."

"Please, Ma'am, where will Cicero and I eat – when the time comes?"

"He knows to come here with his dish and take food to the stable, where he stays. You, my Gull, will eat wherever I need you to be at the time, mostly in the tavern but out of the way of folks. Sometimes hit'll suit to do yer eating here. One of us – Tomm Toliver or I – must be in the tavern at all times, so we eat either here or 'ere as needs be. We make no flutter over meals oursels, as our business is to please 'em what pays to eat at our table."

The water for cleaning and cooking was in a wooden bucket near the fire. Lizzy carefully placed the cut potatoes in an iron pan she had heated already by setting it on red coals she had raked to the side of the fire. Water sizzled as she poured it over the potatoes and put on the lid.

"Now's a time to show ye where ye'ill be warshing of bedclothes and all." Goody was going out the door, motioning to her "Gull," who rushed to keep up.

Outside, three iron wash pots of different sizes were hanging against the kitchen wall beneath a slight overhang of the roof. Lizzy had never seen so much ironmongery as the Tolivers had. There was a fortune in big cooking pots and pans and now these wash pots too. She wondered if they had wagoned them all the way from Pennsylvania.

Seeing the girl's admiration, Goody spoke purr-like, "We got t'ese from a Wilmington merchant who had 'em straight from England. The old ones 'at were here had holes, and we traded 'em in for the value of the iron. 'Tis a hard business to dig out and fire the iron ore in 'ese parts, but 'ere be some 'at do it. Ye must be particular to wipe 'em clean and dry after t'ey cool and turn 'em against the wall, jest so. When you warsh, the boy will lay the fire the evening before and light it under a pot before day. He will put enough water to boil so 'at you can dip out hot water to warsh with and have enough left to boil clothes that need to be boilt. You see the table, for wooden tubs 'at we keep in the kitchen. Do ye know how to make soap, even?"

"Yes, Ma'am," Lizzy was glad to answer, her mother having made different kinds of soaps for cleaning, washing, and also for fulling the cloth she made so that it would be even and smooth to the touch.

"Hummph," Goody shorted. "Then I'll show ye how I make mine when the time comes."

"Are there sheets and coverlids on all the beds?" Lizzy wanted to know.

"Lands, no, we be not throwing money into so much linen for sheets everywhere. Just for the best, don't ye know? Now, coverlids, we do have, serviceable wool goods brought in by the women hereabouts from time to time, in trade for liquors, tea, and other medicinals. Our visitors sleep warm, whether on straw piles or good corn-shuck mattresses."

Lizzy feared to speak about bedbugs, but she knew they were everywhere. "With so many people coming and going, some are bound to carry chinches on them. How do you deal with chinches, Mrs. Toliver?" She hoped her polite words would ease any hard feeling.

"With our bedsteads for the better sort, we set ev'ry bed leg in a dish of turpentine and warsh the sheets right often. For floor-sleepers, it's jest a situation. I offer turpentine for dousing mattresses from time to time. That helps some. Hit keeps off sore throats, too." She shot a sneer Lizzy's way. "Missy Lizzy hersel' will 'deal with chinches' now; mayhap she will make a magic cure."

The New Face

Lizzy did not know what to say and offered to go look about the potatoes. They were soft enough, and she thought about seasoning and browning them. She saw a wide pan with a long handle and looked about for bear grease. She knew it would be easier for the Tolivers to have bear grease than lard for cooking, so Goody would not likely scold her. She had spotted bunches of dried herbs hanging along one wall. Once she had the grease melting in the pan, she pinched down rosemary and tarragon. She dipped the potatoes into the hot grease and rubbed the herbs to powder between her hands over the potatoes. It smelled good. She did not know whether there was any salt. She stirred the potatoes until Goody returned.

Goody said nothing. Together they filled large bowls with the potatoes and beans: "'taties and leather britches," Goody called them. Lizzy was glad to see the larger bowls were pewter and so would not break. One had a few dents, probably from dropping, and the other looked unmarked. The pots on the hearth still held enough food for Cicero and herself.

Delivering the trays gave Lizzy her first sight of the old Red Dog. Four men sat around a table, drinking from worn pewter tankards and shiny clay pots, smoking pipes and lively with talk. They hushed and looked up when the smell of food reached them. Goody and Lizzy put the trays on the bar, and Goody reached for four plates. Wordlessly, she showed Lizzy how much to put in each plate. Goody took two plates at a time to the table, carefully standing at each man's left side while placing a plate before him. She broke the silence placing the last plate. "Good to see ye faces again in the Red Dog, Ginnelmen. My good husband has seen to ye beer pots, and now warm bowls will see ye through the night, I hope."

Lizzy saw another man in the room, his chair pulled sidewise to the small fireplace, reading a newspaper by the firelight. He had looked up when Goody spoke, and he smiled to her as she finished.

"Goodwife, you look well. I'll be staying the night again. When you have the time and inclination, I would welcome your company with the *Virginia Gazette.*"

"Indeed I would, Mr. Marshall," she replied warmly and took a chair near him. "Until another eater comes in, I have time to listen gladly." He began reading the newspaper aloud in a voice that did not reach the men at the table.

"Tomm Toliver," a tall young man with ginger hair called out, "I see a new face at the Red Dog. Whose is the child?"

"She's Lizzy O'Canning, just made our apprentice two day ago. Her . . ."

The young man broke in: "O'Canning. Not any creature-kin of Ned Canning, I hope?" The other men hooted at the name. Lizzy had never heard of Ned Canning and said so.

"*Her* father was *David* O'Canning, Tomm continued, "a Virginia man who drowned in Deep River some ten years back. His widow lived near Richland and was a spinster and weaver of repute. She died just afore Christmas. Lizzy is a goodly gull, and we be proud to have her help. Lizzy, you need to know who 'ese men be, for t'ey often come 'ere," and he said the name of each man about the table for her to hear. She did not expect to remember the names, but she took in their faces and the looks they wore.

When the men had finished eating, she took their plates aside and asked if they wanted more drinks. Only the ginger-haired man did not. She had seen a washbasin and water bucket on a back table, so she washed the plates and spoons. She did not know what she should do next, for the Tolivers had not yet eaten. She asked Tomm if she should go to the kitchen and come back later for the bowls.

"'Course, go and eat ye supper. One of us will bring the bowls."

She did not want to ask about bedding so early, but she was sorely tired.

Back in the kitchen, the leather britches and potatoes tasted good, and she filled herself. Cicero knocked and came in while she ate. He carried a bent-up pewter platter, but it was good and big. He would not take all the food, saying another eater might arrive at the tavern, and besides there was plenty. And there was. Goody intended to work her servants hard, but she would not make them go hungry.

"Do you have something to sleep on?" Cicero asked. "There be clean straw I can bring you."

"Yes, but eat first. Why don't you eat here, and we can go together for the straw and take less time? Four hands, half the work." The boy looked surprised but sat down beside the fire and ate quickly. He did not talk. She took his platter, washed it, and returned it to him. "Let's go get my straw."

They went to the stable and got unused straw from the far end. There was no place for a fire, and as they left, he picked up a piece of crocus cloth. Once they spread the straw in the kitchen where Lizzy wanted it, he showed her the cloth and pointed to a stone in the fireplace.

"That be my warming rock. I wrap it ever' night to stay warm. I bring it back the next day where it will be warm again. You don't mind, do you, Missy?"

"That is clever. I wondered how you kept warm." Then remembering, "Oh, Mrs. Goody wants you to show me how to milk in the morning."

"Yes'm, I 'spect she does. Have yourself a good sleep."

As he left, Lizzy imagined him saying, "You sure going to need it." She banked the fire with ashes and made her way by its dim light to her straw and Aunt Chassie's coverlid.

The next sound was the creaking door and Goody making her noisy way into the kitchen.

"No lying a-bed for ye, Missy. At Toliver's we beat the sun in summer *and* winter. After today, ye'll ready the fire and the mush ever morning. Bring over sticks and a log while I pull back the ashes. And fill pot for boiling. One-two, one-two!"

Goody had brought a pitcher of beer and showed Lizzy how to mix it with the mashed up potatoes and skin and the thick potato water from last night. Goody mixed in meal and flour, using the long wooden trencher to stir and bend the dough so it took up more flour. She took pains about how she did it, and Lizzy wanted to remember. No doubt making some sort of bread would be part of Lizzy's daily work. Goody took down a piece of cloth from a wall-shelf, draped it over the ball of dough, and set the trencher, dough, cloth and all at a particular spot on the hearth.

"How will I know what to do next with the dough, and when?" Lizzy wanted to know.

"'Tis for your eyes and nose to learn. Ye mind close when I work w' it today. Ye can do many t'ings while bread rises, but ye must ne'er forget ye're a-making bread."

Lizzy liked the way Goody busied about, and the way her mushroom eyes talked as much as her mouth did.

Carefully, Goody took down a large piggin and held it low and level so Lizzy could see a deep bowl inside. The bowl was nearly straight-sided, so it fit safely in the piggin. Goody took down a low stool also. "Here. Take 'ese to cow byre. The boy will be 'ere already. Mind ye learn carefully. This will be yourn to do, now on. Be partic'lar to learn how to keep cows from a-kicking. We have no other milking bowl, mind! When you bring in the milk, I will show you what to do with it."

Lizzy finished wrapping on her clothes and shoes, not her best that she had worn to court and the ride here, but older goods for every day.

At the byre near the stable, Cicero had put corn in two troughs, but the cows were still in the stalls. Lizzy reckoned the amount of corn would have to last the whole time a cow was being milked. Cicero seemed to think so, for he showed Lizzy all he could about milking while there was no cow at a trough. He showed her which side of the cow to put the stool, calling it the "near side," and showed her how to sit, guarding the piggin with her left leg in case the cow kicked toward it. "Coo to the cow some before you set your stool. Let her know your voice and your touch, starting at her neck and slowly moving toward her back flank."

"Like with a horse?" Lizzy asked. He nodded.

"Two ways there be to use your fingers. The safe way is to strip down the teat, like this," demonstrating on his left index finger. He used his right thumb and index finger, saying, "More strength at the top, then ease up some coming down. Careful not to pinch. That be the best way to take care of Miz Goody's milking bowl."

"Have you been milking up to now?"

"No'm. Miz Goody been do all the milking. She must trust you fine." Lizzy thought Goody just did not want to milk any more.

"What about the calves?" Two calves were bawling in a stall separate from the cows.

"Get all the milk you can. Cow will hold back some milk for the calf. Get your things out of the way, and then turn the calf in. Miz Goody always milked both cows before she turned their calves loose. The calves will stay with their mammas all day, so there be no milking job at night here. Instead, I will separate the calves from the cows and put 'em in the stalls to stay overnight, like you see 'em now."

It all made sense to Lizzy. "Now we'll see if I can do what you said."

Cicero took the lead and showed her every step, starting with letting the first cow out of her stall. She went straight to the trough, and Lizzy knew her time was running. After she introduced herself to the cow, calling her by name as Cicero told her, she tried to be gentle but bold with her touch. It seemed to take forever before she got a good flow of milk steaming into the bowl. After milking one teat, she was confident enough to try two hands at a time. She felt nervous and stiff. Cicero suggested humming or singing. Lizzy was not sure whether it calmed herself or the cow, but it did go more easily. After she had milked all four teats, Cicero said he thought there was more milk left and she should keep on. Finally, he said she had almost as much milk as Miz Goody always got from this cow. So that's what he's thinking about; good for him, Lizzy thought.

They made it through the second cow, but not before the cow ate all the corn and was bawling for her calf. At the end, Lizzy held onto the piggin with one hand, fearful lest the upset cow would make her lose two cows worth of milking! Being worried and that close to the cows had made her hot. She would remember to remove some wraps tomorrow. She set the piggin aside so she could watch how Cicero let out the calves. That part would not be hard.

In the kitchen, Goody said nothing about what Lizzy thought was a praiseworthy bowlful of milk. Goody made a fuss over how to strain the milk after scalding the next bowl. She even *boiled* the cloth she had strained it through, barking to

Lizzy that if these things were "not done proper-like," the milk would ruin, then there would be no butter for the tables, all would be in disorder, and the world would likely come to an end right here at the Red Dog before the day was done.

Wa'ro

The best thing about finishing the milking, straining it, and cleaning up was that Lizzy now could breakfast. A bit of butter left from yesterday was a treat, stirred in the mush. Maybe the woman's fussy ways with milk were important.

Contentment did not last. Goody informed Lizzy that she had started a stew for the day's fare, and that would leave Lizzy free to scrub down the kitchen and everything in it. Today. All day. Not the old iron pans, though. They would wait until Lizzy could spend another day with a fire outside, baking off the crust from everything on the place that had hard grease baked on it. Goody had told Cicero to get white clay from the hillside. Lizzy knew how to whitewash. It was easier than the big cleaning job that needed doing first. She would be inside, she reminded herself, and there was food. She did not know yet nor care what was in Goody's stew.

Thus Lizzy spent her first full day at the Red Dog scrubbing everything, ev-er-y-thing, in the kitchen. She washed the shelves and hanging rods that held them. Then she went for the walls, which were heavy with soot in some places and with general grime all over. Lye soap, corncobs, and brushes that someone had made from the soft wood of saplings: Lizzy put her strength into the work, wondering if anyone had ever cleaned the kitchen. Certainly not since the Tolivers got it.

He mind ran to the costly "improvements" the Tolivers had made in the place. New buildings and parts of buildings, all that new pewter and ironmongery, chairs and tables that probably were not here when they came. Those things cost money, which for most people meant debt. The thought of debt scared Lizzy. She hoped the Tolivers would have enough visitors to make the money to pay back whatever they had borrowed. They likely sold a farm in Pennsylvania to buy the place, but furnishing and improving it had to be extra expense, to say nothing of the cost of the three cows and two horses she had seen, and Cicero. No wonder Tomm could not afford to buy a Negro girl for Goody! Lizzy felt glad she was not a Negro girl; the thought left her uneasy and puzzled. There was so much she did not know.

Webs of soot and who-knows-what-all hung from the ceiling. She scooted a chair around to get to all the ceiling. Tomm had brought in a long sapling with corn shucks fastened in the bushy end, and she used it to tear down the nastiness. She burned the dirty shucks in the fire, but she saved the sapling and remembered how the shucks had been fastened to it. All that ceiling-sweeping had piled dirt on the floor, so the next thing was to sweep it out, along with all the bits of trash scattered along the hard dirt floor. She would need to sprinkle water on the floor and smooth it down after the sweep-out. Zounds! Would she live long enough to finish the floor and be ready to whitewash?

Cicero brought pails of white clay and water before she finished the floor. He started making a thin white paste to smear on the walls with corn shuck brooms.

"Whooo, you made this wall *clean.* Never see it like this. I'll whitewash it with you, and we be finished before you know it. Where Miz Goody?"

"We took most of her stew to the tavern to have all the day and tonight. Sounds like a crowd of people."

They started in whitewashing, each to a wall. The work was not hard, and talk came easily.

"I want to know about your life before now. Where did you live before Pennsylvania? Where did you live when your mother trained you to grow crops?" Lizzy had not been out of Johnston County since she could recall time. The whole world was new to her.

"I going to say 'Pennsylvania' now, Miss Lizzy, like you. You talk better'n some."

Lizzy laughed, "My mother was careful about that. Do go on."

"The man who took me to Pennsylvania was a trader in Negroes. He had me and eight other people in a big wagon and sold us one or two at a time moving through the country."

"What happened to *your* mother?"

"My mother did not cross the ocean with us. The ship-men left her with some others in the pens."

Lizzy did not understand. "Pens? Please, I do not know anything about how people like you came to be as you are." She did not want to hurt his feelings with her wonderings, but she had to know about this. She asked him timidly if he had always been a slave.

He did not know what she meant.

"Your mother and father, were they free when you first knew time?"

"My father worked with iron. He made tools. Men came to our village and bought them. He was a leading man. He carried the name of our village, our people: Wa'ro." He spoke softly now. "My mother and the other women grew crops, kept animals, made bright colored cloth. We had plenty and good time. That is my first knowing of time."

"How did you get to the pens and the ship-men?"

"Bad neighbors come at night with torches and knives. Many bad men together. They tie us all and herd us like goats to a village of Ashanti people. There be other men there, and they give cattle and iron to the bad neighbors. Then the Ashanti men make us walk much far, across the land we knew and through marshy places, like there be hereabouts, and then through a plain of grasses till we reached the sea. They put us in pens by the sea. Then men with ships take all the healthy people into the ships." He looked very sad and had stopped smearing the whitewash. Lizzy felt her heart ache.

"They left your mother in the pens. Was she sick?"

"She was far along with child."

That is so much worse than my parents dying, Lizzy thought; so very much worse, and so many people.

"The bad neighbors sold your village people to other men, who paid the Ashanti to take you to the pens, and then the ship men bought you at the pens?"

"Yes, it was more selling times than that. I do not know how many times they sell us before we go on the ships."

"Then the ships brought you to Pennsylvania, right?"

"No, no. Many more selling times. After a long time at sea, with many people dying or drowning themselves, we came to an island with people like I had not seen before. We stayed there some days. They divide us and put us onto three more ships. There already people like us on two of them. The ship for me went to a town called Boston. I do not know where the other two went."

"Were any of your village people with you on the Boston ship?"

"Yes, other boys and girls. My sister was with me, my young sister." Lizzy thought of Davo.

"The pens in Boston bigger and cleaner. We bathe and walk about, and they feed us. They want the sick people to get well for more money. That is where the trader buy us nine. My sister not one of them. I did hear a Boston man take her to wait on his family in a big house. Already she know how to make cloth. I wonder do they know that?"

"You are a strong, suffering person, Cicero." She had not said his name before, and it sounded strange, not like him. "Is that your real name?"

He looked hard at her, and both went back to their work. Then he said,

"That be name man in Pennsylvania say to me, and the name he say to Mr. Tomm. It not be my mother-name."

"Will you tell me your real name? I will not tell."

"My name is Wa'ro," he smiled. "The name of my people and my father. I be his eldest."

Lizzy thought about all that. Could it ease any of his sorrow to have even a part of his own name to keep?

"Ro. . . Ro! I can call you Ro," she burst out. "Don't you hear it? ' Ro is short for Wa'ro, and it's the last part of Cicero too!"

She was afraid he would think her foolish, but her excitement caught his spirit.

"I'll call you "Ro' in a natural way, and no one will think anything."

Wa'ro grinned. They had finished all the whitewashing.

The Petition

Lizzie thought the Tolivers might need her in the tavern, for she heard horses and shouts of arrival. After eating some of the stew Goody had left, she cleaned her hands, arms, and face, quickly washed her linen kerchief, bonnet, and apron and lay them before the fire to dry. Lye soap cleaned well, but her hands hurt from using so much today. A little bear grease eased them, and with fresh linen goods and a full stomach, she headed for the public room.

Glad to see her, Tomm sent her back to the cellar to bring all the buttermilk she could carry. Then Goody had her bring the last big loaf of raised bread and corn pone and also four onions. The visitors had eaten "every tuck of my stew," Goody said, and would "finish the night out with homely fare." Lizzy heard a young voice cry out, "'Twas goodly stew, Missus, 'twas, with as homely-tasting possums as ever slid through my maw."

There must have been 30 men in the room, plus a knot of women near the door. Lizzy kept hearing words sounding like "vestry," "privilege," "parish," "rector," "marry," and "stablishment." Mostly the talk sounded angry. People kept looking at a paper on a side table, with a quill and inkpot beside it. The crowd seemed to favor it, and Lizzy could see where men had signed it, some writing their names and some writing an initial or a cross. She knew that people who could not write their names wrote a cross, like to say they were Jesus'. She wondered what the paper said, but she dared not venture to go close.

Soon her ears told her what her eyes could not reach. She was behind the bar next to Tomm, washing and wiping pots and tankards for him to fill, when two men entered and made their way through the crowd to ask for a drink. One also asked, "Tavernier, what is this hubbub? Be that a piece of politics on yon table?"

"So it be, good stranger, and welcome. For stranger ye must be not to know of it. Zack here can speak it," pointing his head toward an older man further back from the bar. Lizzy wondered if Tomm did not want to talk about it or if he was just too busy pouring locust beer.

"Where do you live, strangers, and where are you going?" the old man asked.

"We are of Ebenezer, in Georgia, on our way to brethren in Pennsylfania. I am Ordman, and this is Fryermuth. We haff a long journey and vish to spend a peaceful night here. But, please, what is it that excites so?"

The old man, having plenty of time, a full beer pot, and a steady bench beneath him, motioned them to sit. He set about his talk,

"The mighty men near our coast, with their plantations and ocean trade -- they use this colony's Assembly to gain riches for themselves and the handful of friends they have here in the back parts. Most members of the Assembly are eastern men. There be many small counties near the ocean, and counties in these here parts are new, few, and big. The Assembly works with their lawyer and merchant friends who move here -- to the backcountry -- and take up our county offices. They be worse further west than in this county. Different sorts of mischief come from this partnering between courthouse people and the Assembly. Many mischiefs."

"Vaat is the problem this night?" The stranger was puzzled.

"Well, ye see, the people here tonight be worked up about a new law that is expected the Assembly will pass. Five times they have lawed it that we all over North Car'liny pay taxes to feed the Anglican ministers. We say them that goes to that church pay for it. Did you know that Anglican ministers are the only preachers can marry a couple, be that man and 'oman Dutch, Presbytern, re-baptizers, silly Quakers, or regular heathen. Anglican folk be scarcer than rabbit horns here in the backcountry. We say all preachers should marry their own sort of people and whoever seeks them out that be lawful to marry. That be the heart of the paper on the table yonder."

The stranger who had talked turned to the other and spoke for some time in a language Lizzy had not heard. She was amazed.

"Ye be Dutch, do ye, in this Ebenezer?" Zack lit up.

"From Salzburg. Our settlement is 30 years old. Good Colonel Oglethorpe himself vanted us to move there, and ve fare vell. Ve have visits from German settlements in the Upcountry parts of South Carolina, and on occasion Herr Bolzius stays with us on his preaching journeys. A godly man. He comes from the towns in the Vachau: Wachovia in English. Do you know the place?"

"Never have I been there, but I know them that has. A curious place. I hear its church runs everything, but they are not in the 'stablished church. Most curious to us here."

Lizzy had to step away to fetch more thing to wash, but she hurried back. She still had not heard what the paper on the table said. Another man had joined the two strangers and Zack, and he was talking about the people in Wachovia. He was the man who had shared a newspaper with Goody last night.

"They are 'Moravians,' of the Unitas Fratrum, from Moravia in Europe, and they came to this colony from Pennsylvania," he was saying and added, "as have many. They are Protestants like us, but with some forebears even earlier than Martin Luther." Turning to the visitor who spoke English, he asked, "Are your Salzburg people of Luther?"

"Most assuredly." He added, "and of the Saviour."

Zack wanted to know how the Moravians could have their own church and pastors marrying but not pay for Anglican ministers. "Mo-ravians be in North Car'liny, like the rest of us. Are they fussing up about the vestry law that's coming? Do they have men in the Assembly that cousin with the coastal lawyers and all? What is their secret, Mr. Marshall?"

Marshall waited a moment for the Georgia man to translate to his friend.

"The Moravians do have a special arrangement with the Assembly. They got it worked out before they moved down here. As our friends from Ebenezer know, the people who run a colony that has an Indian frontier want to have white people in good numbers near that frontier. The Moravians in this colony, the Salzburgers in Georgia, the Dutch Fork people and other German-speakers in western South Carolina: legislatures made special deals to get them to settle there – to be a brace against Indians."

The German visitor translated, and his companion nodded agreement.

"You mean like cheap land? Where does religion come in?" Zack wanted to know.

"First of all, the settlers cannot be papists, in case the Spanish or French side with frontier Indians against a colony, like in the Cherokee War just past. If the church leaders are canny enough, they can state what they want in the way of local control. That is what the Moravians did more than ten years ago. A new vestry law is not likely to bother them, because Wachovia already is its own parish with its own vestry, though the Moravians don't call it that. They call it a German name. It does not mean anything new. It is just the way they already did things, but set up as a pretend parish, so to speak. This makes it look on paper like the Moravian Church is the Anglican Church in Wachovia. But of course it is not."

The German seemed not to need to explain this to his friend, like it was something he knew already.

Zack on the other hand was agog. "Mr. Marshall, you do get about the country." Then, "Do the Mo-ravians send their own people to the Assembly, or do they have to use easterners' lackeys like other places in the back parts?"

Lizzy did not get to hear the answer, because Goody motioned to her from the fireside across the room, and she went there along the wall to avoid going through the crowd of men. Goody had made sassafras tea in a pot hanging over the fire, and it smelled wonderful. She was filling small pottery bowls on a tray and told Lizzy to take them "to the women that be gossiping by the door nook," so Lizzy did.

As she expected, the women looked Lizzy over – up, down, and sideways – while she stood to the right of each of them to set down their steaming bowls. Mother had taught her that: "Food from the left, drink from the right, a well-placed dish is the eyes' delight."

"My, ye be a young thing to work a public house, dearie. And who might ye be?"

"I am newly apprenticed here, Ma'am." When she said her name, there came the question she had heard already: "ye've nothing to do with Ned Canning, I trust?" How word got around on that man!

"I know him not. Please, who might he be?"

"No one a young gull wants to have around her," pronounced a bobbing head under a soiled bonnet that stood out from a wool wrap. The next woman spoke plainly, however.

"Pshaw! He is a rascal come here from the north colonies, New York likely. He and partners set up a trading company at Childsborough, or Hillsborough, or whatever name it has at this moment: the court town on the Eno River." She stopped for breath and went on. "They're making it a den of pettifogging lawyers, so my husband says. Merchants calling in debts before their time and taking every feather and fowl to court to strip them of their mites, down to the last louse and its nits. Shameful! Word is that three years ago Canning came in with a little money borrowed from his cousins who trade in the Virginia ports. Right off got to be the big man of Orange County. His friends in the Assembly put him in as a town commissioner for Hillsborough and an officer of the county court. The governor appointed him register of deeds and I don't know what-all. These government jobs give him excuses to wring money from honest folk." She sniffed and went right on.

"And it's his sort that's getting up laws to pinch out the few preachers who live hereabouts or who journey here from time to time. We need them for the Lord's Supper, for baptizing, and for marrying all that wants to marry."

The face on the bobbing head winced. "Well, Molly Strickland, ye be full of phlegm on this subject, ain't ye? Myself, I want to be knowing about this young person. Lizzy, be ye an orphan, or be ye the devil's spawn from a whore? Tell me your people – if you know."

Lizzy thought Goody might need her again, but she did not want to run away from this sharp tongue.

"My mother was Mrs. Elizabeth O'Canning, and she raised my brother and me by spinning and weaving as nice linen and wool as ever was made. She died just lately. I hardly remember my Papa, for he died when I was but three. Mr. Justice of the Peace Buchannon was a neighbor and helped me to a place here." She spoke these words as though the Red Dog were a palace. After all, it had attracted all these people this night, and soon it would have a Manor House.

"My," the face drew back, her hand to her cheek, "at least ye poor mother taught ye to speak and comport yourself mannerly. Hummph. Ye may be a credit to the Tolivers. They can use it."

Now that the confrontation had ended, Lizzy looked to see if Goody was watching. She was not, so Lizzy ventured to ask what she would not have asked the men she had listened to.

"Since I am new here," she began meekly, "would you tell me what is that paper on the table, and why are some men signing it?" As she expected, the one called Molly was quick to speak.

"It is a petition against a new law that is intended in the Assembly when it meets in New Bern next. The big eastern men have passed laws like it before, to make sure their preachers are the only lawful ones in all o' North Carolina, but the king rejected those laws. Not that he would be against their idea! The lawyers just didn't get the legal words right, my husband said, so the king said no." She breathed twice and continued, "Most folk hereabouts be Dissenters, you see, such as we Baptists, and Presbyterians, and Quakers and New Lights and all. That runs against the law that the only proper church in a royal colony is the Church of England, or Anglican as is called. It not be right that Dissenters pay tax to pay salaries of Anglican preachers. We want to support our own clergy. It not be right that the only clergy who can marry a man and a woman in this colony be an Anglican. We want our own preachers to marry us. Besides, it be easier to find one of our'n that travels through the backcountry. Anglican ministers rarely visit these parts. To have only one kind of church be legal – why, that don't suit us here, no mor'n it suited our grandparents or their Dissenter people in Old England afore our folks came over here. No. No. No. The petition is a letter to the Assembly saying we don't want that law. Myself, I made it my business to come here tonight to watch and see what men sign it. I believe most will, what with folk watching and all."

Another woman spoke. "We four got it up that we would come and just drink 'fras and watch. Got it up last Sabbath, we did. Naught wrong with married women being here, quiet-like and out of the way, when their men-folk have important matters to tend. That be what Mr. Marshall his own self allowed."

"Shall I fill your dishes again, ladies?" They nodded contentedly, and Lizzy returned to the hearth knowing a great deal more than before this evening.

The Skin Trader and his 'Neech'

Lizzy got used to working for the Tolivers sooner than she thought she would. But she did not get used to being without Davo. Every day she jolted awake wondering how he was, if he was safe, if the man Leetch was too hard on him, if he had ague or some other distemper in this cold weather, all the things that ran to her mind. At night when she fell asleep, after she was thankful for what she had to be thankful for, she prayed about Davo and tried then to calm herself and not imagine bad things.

She had to find a way to know about him. Tomm seemed pleased with how Lizzy was doing, and Goody had fewer complaints and outbursts than she might have had, so Lizzy hoped it would not be long before she could ask how she could get up to where Davo was, to see about him. She thought it would be no longer a road than what she and Tomm had taken from the courthouse, and that it would be easier because there would not be streams, once she got across the river at the easy ford near here. Such thoughts always were in her mind.

Not that she had time to think about much more than work! The good thing was, though, that she got used to some of the work and sometimes could free her mind while she did it. She could not drift off while milking, that was sure. She was getting along with the cows all right. The calves seemed to have something against her, and she could understand that; she was stealing their milk. She petted them some while they sucked their mammas, and they were getting used to her. At least she was not the one to separate them at night. Wa'ro had that job.

Lizzy called him 'Ro two times when he was not around. The first time, both Tolivers heard it, and Tomm looked at her. So she said, "That name 'Cicero' is a mouthful. ' Ro' is easier" and shrugged. She had no call to say his name much, anyway, and next time she said it, it was to Goody, asking if 'Ro could take the ashes out to the hopper at the wash place today instead of Lizzy because she was all caught up in changing Goody and Tomm's bedroom and cleaning their floors. Goody just said, "all right."

Some of Lizzy's jobs were regular, every day, and she felt easy about them. Most of them were in the morning or around dinner and supper and after supper when she did things about food and getting it to the public house. Some days, though, Goody brought on a big job that took all day, and she had to do it on top of the morning jobs. Washing was a bear. Lizzy knew it would be, because washing always was. Goody acted like she was helping at first, but really she was just bossing. 'Ro built up the fire early and placed the heavy pot. He brought up water from the creek and filled the pot, too. That was a powerful lot of help. She did the rest of it herself: taking hot water to smaller pots, scrubbing, boiling some things, hauling water for the rinsing, then rinsing everything twice, laying it out on clean spots or fences to dry, cleaning it all up, folding everything just right and bringing it in. Most of what she washed did not need ironing. The big things were sheets. The nastiness on those sheets shocked Lizzy, whose mother's bedclothes had never looked like that. Goody had said quality people got the room with sheets on the bed! Mayhap Goody had just been lazy about changing and washing sheets. Lizzy was glad some visitors slept on straw like she did. One of these days, she knew, she would have to open the corn shuck mattresses, burn the shucks (with bedbugs and she-knew-not-what in them) and boil the mattress ticks. That would be a devilish job, and she knew she would be the one to put fresh dry shucks back in the ticks and sew them up again after the ticks dried. Oh, yes, attending to bedding was one of her big day-long jobs, like that first day of cleaning and whitewashing the kitchen had been.

On afternoons when Lizzy did not have all-day jobs, Goody or Tomm would put her to odd jobs just for that day, like that afternoon she was helping Tomm clean up from an unusually heavy crowd at dinner, and in came another passel of hungry men. As she brought in more food from the kitchen, Wa'ro came in the back of the Red Dog.

"Mr. Tomm, that skinny hunter-man from over near Spoil Caney be here with four horse loads of deer skins, saying you be to pay him 'fore I unloads them. I know you don't regular do it that way, and 'sides, the skin store-room needs your opening it."

"Here, take the key on and unlock, but don't let 'im unload till Lizzy gets there. Lizzy, I have to stay here. You go tell the man I'll pay him after you satisfy me that the horses be fully packed and the skins be sound. You can do that for me, Gull."

Lizzy would do more than look at the load. She aimed to count the skins as well. When she got to the building where skins were locked in, Wa'ro already had the door open and was telling the hunter that "Miss Lizzy" would "inspect the load."

Lizzy had not seen the man before and realized he did not know she was a servant. He had long black hair tied with a piece of leather, and he was indeed skinny. He was hollering at 'Ro about how to unload the skins and then motioned to a boy about Lizzy's age. He wore brown wool trousers and a hunting shirt with beads on the fringes. A band of beadwork held his straight black hair neatly in place. The man cursed him and told him to get to work unpacking the skins.

"Mr. Toliver sent me to deal with you," she announced, "and I will help them move the skins." Lizzy wanted to count the skins without the man noticing, and she could do that if she worked with the boys. Lizzy was good with numbers, always had been.

"Now, Miss, no need for you to work. You stay by me and give me a little talk. Why, we got us a 'Neech and a Neeg to do the work." When he walked closer and Lizzy caught his scent, she wanted even more to help unload.

"Thank you, but I'll see to the unloading for Mr. Toliver." Clearly, the man was not going to help unload, which was fine with her, and there was no more talk about getting paid first.

At first, the man sat on a sunny stump and idly watched them. When she got a chance, she told 'Ro and the Indian she was counting the skins and not to load too fast, and both nodded. She was keeping a total in her head, but she did not like the man watching. Before long, he sauntered off toward the Red Dog, muttering something about Old Tomm owing him a drink.

Still holding the number in her head, Lizzy slowed down and said to the boy, "I am Lizzy, and this is 'Ro. What is your name, please, and what is the name of the hunter? Mr. Toliver did not tell me."

He looked sidewise at her but not sneaky-sideways. "Buckhorn is my name. Mr. Travers is no hunter. He trades with my people for our deerskins. My brother bought knives, a gun, and whiskey from him sixteen moons ago, but Travers did not give us the old price for our half-dressed skins when he came for them."

"Half-dressed?"

"Our women clean and scrape the skins from our winter hunt, and that brings a higher price. Until this last time! Travers priced our skins like they were un-dressed, said that's all he was buying now. So the value he put on them was less than what our people had bought in the fall." Buckhorn stretched his back as he talked. "Travers said he knew the sheriff in Hillsborough and he would get one of the new lawyers there to get everything my family had for the debt."

That got Lizzy's full attention, and she put down her skins, barely remembering the number.

"So what happened?"

"It may have been a white man's bluff about the sheriff and lawyer, but Travers told my brother he would take me to work for him for two years to pay the debt and keep the sheriff away."

'Ro spoke next. He too had put down his skins to listen. "Hillsborough? All your people I know about live east of here. Where do you live?"

"We have some Saponi people where you speak of, but we are of Occaneechi. We live on what white men call the High Ground, more to the west than Hillsborough is, high up between the Haw and the Eno, north of the white settlements."

They went back to carrying skins and stacking them in the skin house. Now that Travers was not there, 'Ro and Buckhorn made sure Lizzy could count as they stacked, and they kept on talking. She had counted 119 dry skins so far, and the boys had laid aside twelve skins to dry out from where water had got to them. Lizzy wondered where they had crossed Mother Crabtree. Buckhorn told them Travers was buying goods to sell as he got money for skins. They had left a wagon of skins with a merchant in Hillsborough and would get the wagon when they went back. Travers aimed to trade with Tomm for whiskey and take it across the river and up to Osborne's. Travers aimed to buy trade goods at Osborne's. He was buying and selling everywhere he stopped.

Lizzy jumped at the name Osborne! "Is that Big Jeff Osborne's place you're going to?"

"I think. Don't know any other big trader by that name. He and Travers have traded before, and some of my people in the High Ground know Big Jeff Osborne. They say he used to come there regular until he let Travers work for him. That is all I know."

"My brother works somewhere near Osborne's, at a wagon maker or wheelwright this side of Osborne's, name of Leetch. I do not know the area, as I am new here. My brother and I were apprenticed as orphans the first of the year. Please listen or look out for him. I am so worried. He is only nine." Lizzy was rushing her words, not caring at all that Buckhorn knew she was an apprentice.

He looked surprised. "How old are you?"

"Thirteen years."

"Same as me. My ears and eyes will be as a deer's. I do not know if I will be here again. What is his look and how is he called?"

"David O'Canning, likely called Dave. He has yellow hair, as straight as yours, and he is little for his age. Thank you. Even if you don't see me again, you can tell him where and how I am. It would be a comfort to him and a kindness to me."

She wished someone could somehow contact 'Ro's sister in Boston, but that was not likely, and she did not speak of it. Their job done, the boys headed the horses and wagon toward the stable, and Lizzy took her report to Tomm.

Unexpected Skill

The total was 172 skins, counting the ones spread out to dry. She did not include 17 skins she refused because they had spoiled from being wet too long.

"Four beasts and only 172 skins?"

"Did he promise a certain number? I'm sure I counted right."

"Right smart of ye to count, Gull. No number, but I expected summat more'n two hundred for four packhorses."

"They're what the Occaneechi boy with Travers called 'half-dressed,' if that's important." She added, "But Travers allowed only the value of undressed skins when he collected them."

"Well, now, that be right interesting. I see I can dicker with Travers. Hummph. I'll not pay him half-dressed price, not myself. Good Gull, good Gull, Lizzy."

"Begging your pardon, Sir, but the boy said Travers was to get whiskey from you for the skins. I didn't know you had extra whiskey and all, enough to trade out. How does that work?"

Tomm looked sharp at her and then mumbled, "I be to train ye in taverning, so I'll let ye know. The building close by the tavern, I keep it locked too, it be my whiskey house. I keep it in oak barrels 'at I bring into the Red Dog one at a time, like my cider. This time of year I still have enough to trade out. Even if I had the hard coins, I'd keep more value to trade the whiskey for Travers's skins than to pay him money. He'll likely trade some of my whiskey to Big Jeff, who sells a lot more than I do. I aim to wagon his skins, along with other t'ings folks have traded to me, over to Cross Creek. Generally do that once a year. It'll ship out through Wilmington, and go God knows where. Deerskins are like money while 'ey're being traded, and the last merchant 'at handles 'em, he makes the biggest profit."

"Why doesn't Travers take them to Cross Creek?"

"Through here be about as far east as a trader like him is likely to go. He's on a circuit, don't ye know, with big stops at Osborne's and Hillsborough and piddling places like here, too, trying to trade 'up' at every stop. You say he gave 'undressed' value for 'half-dressed skins' from the Occaneechi?"

Before Lizzy could speak, he went on, "Waal, I see I don't give him 'half-dressed' value in his whiskey. Ye stay inside behind the bar, Gull. Crowd's slowed down, and Goody's got yer dishes back to the kitchen. I'll dicker wi' Snake Travers while he still feels from 'at drink I gave 'im."

"Sir, I don't know how you keep track of who buys what in here, and I need to." Surely Tomm had some record. But he couldn't tell her anything that she could follow. As he sputtered on about "sums" and "drams" and "whole dinners" and "livery," she got the notion that Tomm was keeping track of what he served his customers without writing anything. The thought made her head hurt. Counting skins was simple compared to this. Fortunately, only a few men left while she was on duty, and they told her what they had bought, as Tomm said they would. She only hoped that Tomm's presence at the far end of the room kept them honest. If this were her public house, she would find a way to record every sale. Paper was scarce, but with enough old linen rags, or even new linen like her mother had grown, she could make paper if she had one of those frames. She bet 'Ro could make a good frame, with all the spare lumber and horsehair there was around here!

When Travers left the room, Tomm rejoined Lizzy, smiling all the way. "I made it stick with him just how many gallons of whiskey he'd get for those skins ye counted. Little Lizzy saved me some profit, and I thank 'ee."

She still didn't understand the whole deal and asked, "Will he get a whole barrel, and how will he get it on a horse?"

"Oh, no, not a full barrel!" E's going now over to the potter up Swift Creek to buy the jugs he needs. Whitby Lincoln and his gulls keep a good stock of jugs made up and ready to sell. That be best t'ing to do with the clay along 'ere. Good and thick and hard-fired. Lincoln pots'll stand up to horse-travel and not lose a drop, I'll wager. Some o 'em jugs will end up in the High Ground when Snake sells the last of my whiskey."

The room was near empty now, and while Lizzy went about gathering the few dishes and tankards, she asked more questions. Tomm was in a good mood with her, so she felt bold.

"Sir, where do you get enough whiskey to sell here and also buy skins?"

"I make the reg'lar whiskey. I have places on springs near about. Bought me some good distilling pieces when we first moved here. We couldn't make a go of it if we had to buy ever't'ing we sell to drink. Goody has a fine hand for distilling, not just me. Whiskey's a grand draw at a place like 'is, second only to the location. We sell good whiskey, as good as any our folks made back in Ireland. Scots who come here from 'eir settlements allow its goodness, too. Oh yes, Tomm and Goody's distilling be the pride of the Red Dog. The foreign spirits, of course, we have to buy and wagon in here – rum, Madeira, and such-like. Peach brandy? Well it comes in here from our neighbors and soon disappears. Cider is more plenteous, but it has a shorter life, goes sour after a while, and that's our vinegar. Not a loss. A body needs vinegar to stay well and all. We make a little cider here, but we buy the most of it from the best orchards and cidery in this part of the colony – the Widow McBee's."

Surprised, Lizzy asked, "Is the Widow McBee's place near here?"

"Not as close as Cicero and I wish it were," Tomm replied with a grin Lizzy did not understand.

"Up near the Tarr River. Wagon takes about t'ree hours, and longer to get back w' the load. I send Cicero 'ere on his own now, and he spends the night, comes back next day." Tomm looked confidential-like at Lizzy. "Cicero's sweet on a gal at the widow's. He says she's one of the main ones who has the secret of making good cider. I doubt Mrs. McBee will ever sell that gal, valuable as she is for what she's doing, so Cicero has no cause for worry there." Lizzy did not comment, but she reckoned 'Ro and the girl had plenty to worry about, just being enslaved.

"I see you have a lot more drink on your price list on the wall, things you don't sell. Why is that?"

"What? Oh, the posted prices. That be what the county court tells us to charge. They do 'at once a year. Jest changed the prices a while back. I have to go by new prices but I've not changed 'e sign. Not had time, don't ye know?"

"I can do it if you like."

"How be yer handwrite, Missy?"

"You can judge. Tell me the first price to write."

Not quite believing her, Tomm reached in a drawer and handed her a list. "Write 'Bill of Fare' at the top, and we'll see. Just write it aside the old one, and ye can paint over it later."

She read the list silently, then peered at the blank wall. "It would look fair to whitewash a block on the wall and then paint the letters with soot oil. Is that possible?"

"'Course it be. Goody keeps a little clay by the warshstand, and I'll make up soot oil agin it's dry." Tomm seemed more confident of her "handwrite" now.

Soon she had written "Bill of Fare" in letters the size Tomm wanted, and he was eager for her to paint more. It took less than an hour for her to copy the notice from the court:

West India Rum per gallon	*13s. 4*
New England Rum per gallon	*10s. 8*
Brandy per gallon	*10s .8*
Madeira Wine per quart	*4s.*
Crab Cider per gallon	*2s.8*
Common Cider per gallon	*1s. 4*
Dinner	*1s.*
Breakfast	*.8*
Supper	*.8*
Lodging per night	*.4*
Indian corn per gallon	*.8*
Oats per gallon	*.8*
Fodder per pound or bundle	*.1*
Toddy per quart with West India Rum & L.S.	*1s. 4*
Toddy per quart with New England Rum or Brandy	*1.*

Tomm watched at her side, his blue eyes big with excitement. She had more questions.

"Sir, what does 'L.S.' mean with the West Indies toddy?"

Tomm was proud to answer: "Loaf Sugar. Sugar makes 'e price higher than the New Englander. Same with the crab cider. Takes sugar for the crab apple."

"Why do they use crab apples? Is it because there are not enough sweet apples?"

"Crab cider is a point of pride, particularly in Virginny. Makes a lighter drink."

"You serve more beer than anything else, but it's not on the list."

"Well, ye see, the purpose of the court list is to keep a lid on 'e prices, so tavern-keepers don't squeeze travelers 'at be here, hungry, thirsty, and tired, with no other public house near about. Everybody sells beer at the same price anyway, depending on what it's made from. A feller gets beer wi' his meal without paying separate. Or a little tea or mayhap some sort or coffee."

Lizzy mused further. "So, if a man were the frugal sort and willing to forgo a special drink for himself but took good care of his horse, he could get by spending about two shillings? He could sup, spend the night, breakfast, and have his horse fed oats at night and fodder in the morning, all for 25 pence, which is two shillings plus one penny, or, as we say, 'two and one.'"

"Indeed, Gull, indeed." Then, his eyes even wider: "You can cypher!? You can read, and write – and *cypher?* And you a poor orphan gull?"

Lizzy stood tall. "My mother taught me as long as she was able. There is much more to learn. But yes, I can work with numbers. And I think I can help you and Mrs. Goody keep up with what people are drinking and eating in here so that they pay you the right amount." She paused to see his reaction and spoke more slowly. "We need paper in the Red Dog, paper to keep accounts on. I know how to keep up with sales, and I know how to make paper. We'll need a frame for paper-making. 'Ro can make one. We have everything we need here."

"Goody! Good, Good Wife! Gudrun!" He ran toward the kitchen, leaving Lizzy to add at the bottom of their Bill of Fare sign: *By order of the court of Johnston County.*

Gudrun's Tale

Lizzy expected Goody to rail and frail against the notion of making paper and recording sales, but Tomm's belief that they would make more money that way won her over. It helped, too, that the trading with Snake Travers had given the Tolivers a clear profit. It put Goody in a friendlier mood than Lizzy had seen. She began to understand what had attracted Tomm to her besides her flash looks.

Goody was all smiles when she and Tomm came back. They brought a mess of beans and bacon from the kitchen for the three of them. With no one else in the Red Dog, they settled into a comforting meal together. To Lizzy, it felt so much like a family that it made her happy and sad at once. The feeling shocked her.

Goody wanted to make sure the girl did not misunderstand. "Ye'ill still be milking and helping sommat in kitchen, and fetching food and dishes back and forth to the Red Dog, and warshing, but I guess ye can spend some of yer afternoons and evenings in the Red Dog with 'ese new doings. Jest so ye know ye're not to be a full time queen of the public house, so to say." Lizzy could not imagine how she could keep on doing all her regular work and spend more time in the Red Dog too. They knew her value now, so she would not worry about the work.

Goody having made her speech, she relaxed into her meal, washing it down with what Lizzy thought was an extra amount of sumac beer. Lizzy was drinking sassafras tea she had minded herself, so it was not strong and bitter. It would not do to use enough sugar to make bitter tea fit to drink.

Tomm had poured hot 'fras into his tankard and added sumac beer to it. "Ye've outdone yersel, Goody, with this new batch. Some sumac beer is too tart to hold in yer mouth, but this is light and fine. We won't miss 'e locust, now that it's gone. A fine brew, this, me Love."

Goody beamed, saying nothing.

Before Lizzy thought, she asked what she had long wanted to know. "Mrs. Goody, I like that name for you, but is 'Goody' your Christian name?" Shocked by her own words, Lizzy looked aside and chewed her beans carefully.

"I be proud to say that my 'Da was a sailor man who saw many shores. He heered my name first in the far north, in the Faroe Islands. He was a lad at the time."

"Tell the gull where the Faroes be, Goody."

"Ah, a long way off from his home in Ireland. 'Da said it was halfway between the tip-top of Scotland and *Iceland.*"

"Iceland?" Lizzy startled. "I heered tell of Iceland. It sounds mighty cold. What time of year was he there?"

"Ah now, that be part of the story." Goody seemed pleased to tell more. "'Twas the end of the summer trading season. My 'Da and his mates worked out of Hull in England. The captain wanted to make one last run to Norway before the weather set in and hired them that were willing to stay on for extra pay. On the way back, they got in a storm for days but ended up on one of the Faroe Islands. As near an escape as ever was, he allowed. The vessel spent the winter there, but the men couldn't do much repair until spring. They did what they could to help the folks there: mending nets and ropes indoors by the fire, tending animals in the byre-room of the house. The talk was foreign, nothing like people in Ireland talked, either in Gaelic or English. The sailors were quick to learn, though. It was an adventure all right. 'Da said the place turned just beautiful next summer, after the vessel was fixed and they could leave."

"And was there someone there called 'Goody'?"

"One of t'ree gulls in the village named 'Gudrun.' It was a popular name, comes from old stories. That was what my 'Da said he liked best about 'at winter: hearing the stories 'ey told, like people do, I guess, everywhere, but t'ese were different stories from ones he heered in Ireland. He said t'ere were stories late into the night ever' night and he never heard the same one twicet. Magical, it was. T'is gull Gudrun was one of the storytellers. She liked my 'Da, but she was not of a mind to leave home. Particularly with a stranded, penniless sailor, come to think on it." Goody smiled to think of her father young and unmarried.

"So later he named you for this Gudrun?"

"Not exactly. *She* was named for a Gudrun in some of the old stories he heered. That Gudrun, way back in time, was a fierce woman and not to be tampered with."

Lizzy waited for more. She glanced at Tomm, who looked like he knew there would be more and was glad of it.

"So this Gudrun of the stories was a heroine, like?"

"My, yes, but a very hard woman." It crossed Lizzy's mind that Goody might think of herself that way.

"Now, this Gudrun had to marry a mean man. It was not her choice. Her mother bossed her into it. He was a cruel man, name of Att-ily-Hun. He killed just anybody, or sent others to do it. One by one he killed . . . ." Goody's eyes were on their mushroom stems again, and Lizzy's backbone went all tight. "One by one, I say, that man Att-ily-Hun killed ever'body in Gudrun's family. He thought t'ey had gold. There was naught left but *her.*"

Lizzy wondered if Goody remembered that Lizzy's parents were dead, but the thought faded as the story went on.

"Gudrun filled herself with a tremor of revenge. She and old Att-ily-Hun had two little boys. Ye won't believe 'eir names, funny names: Erp and Idle. Sounds like one allus had indigestion and the othern was just lazy, eh? I donno. But 'em boys was the whole world to Att-ily-Hun. And you know what Gudrun done?"

Lizzy was afraid to ask.

"She *killed* 'em and cut 'em up in a stew, made a real feast of it, as meat was scarce. She seasoned it with yarbs she had a-growing in all the windowsills, and Att-ily-Hun swore he'd never tasted anything so good. Well, he hadn't, ye know? Nothing was as good as his own little boys. Now, 'at Gudrun, she done 'at because she had willed up a tremor of rage. It made her different from her ordinary self. Folks can do that, ye know. Hummph."

The story couldn't be over!

"What did Att-ily-Hun do to her?"

"It's what she did to *'im.* He took to bed in 'is sorrow, and she thrust a knife into 'im and then *burned down the whole place.* Att-ily-Hun and all his men died.

"But Gudrun still didn't have any people."

"No, Child. She didn't. She took to the woods, all wild and distracted. She already had a habit of doing that from being so unhappy. She decided to drown herself. Grabbed all 'e big rocks she could, tied 'em 'round her w' her apern and walked into the sea."

"Ohhh. That's so sad an ending."

"'Tis not quite the end, but might as well be. The sea would not accept her, kept throwing her back to land. Finally she quit trying and just died of her grief."

"Was she ever happy in her life?" Lizzy was wondering why so many people named daughters for poor Gudrun.

"Ah, yes, she had been happy. Happy. She adored her first husband, name of Sigurd, and their little girl. But them two got lost in a storm. Gudrun found his body, but never the little'un. Sunilda was her name. Gudrun's forever-lost daughter. That was a whole other story. Those old stories are all tied together, ye know, going from adventure to adventure and love to sorrow to love again."

Tomm spoke. "'Good entertainment, 'tis. And you tell it well, my Gudrun."

That night when Lizzy went to bed, she felt easier about being with the Tolivers. The time at supper had been so good. She only wished 'Ro could have been part of it. Or at least that Buckhorn could have spent the night with 'Ro and they could be friends. Travers probably took Buckhorn to the pottery to load up the horses. At least 'Ro had a friend at the Widow McBee's. That was a piece of news. She even was hopeful about finding Davo, now that she would be in amongst the public in the Red Dog. Once she learned who was who, she could start asking questions that might lead her to Little Brother.

At Potter Lincoln's

Lizzy was right about Travers taking Buckhorn to Lincoln's for pots. They got there about sundown. Buckhorn had convinced the trader to cross higher on the creek than he wanted to, but the extra time had paid off when the horses took the stream in stride, each man leading one animal and riding another. Buckhorn liked the boy and girl back at Toliver's. They were smart. The boy knew a lot about the surroundings,

Buckhorn could tell. And the girl, well she was not like most white girls he had seen, not that he had seen that many. She seemed to look on him as just another person, not someone to stay away from or be scared of. Same way she treated the boy, 'Ro. She was a servant, 'Ro was a slave, and Buckhorn, well he was a servant too. It seemed like they all should have a chance.

One thing Buckhorn was sure of: when he finished the time Travers had cheated his family out of, he was going back to the High Ground where everybody was the same. The few white women he had known had been in the High Ground, and they acted like the girl at Toliver's, looked you straight in the face, spoke plainly, and expected no special treatment. His uncle was married to one of them, Filipena. She and her brother Ludvig had been servants. She said they came from "Alemania," or something like that, and had been sold when they got off the boat at the Chesapeake. They worked in Portsmouth until they learned enough English to pass for free, then ran off together for the backcountry, walking all night and sleeping in woods during the day. Some of the High Ground people found them after the "road" gave out and only the people who lived there knew how to get about. Filipena and her brother found mates in the High Ground. They added their Portsmouth English to the talk there, along with some words from Alemania. There were a few people who looked like 'Ro there too, some of them elders. It was a good place to live, the High Ground.

The pot-making place was interesting. The road near the place was wide and worn from people coming for dirt dishes and jugs. It was near dusk when they got there, but Buckhorn could see the half-underground hump where they baked the pots, along with stacks of wood. Piles of brush were nearby, and he learned next day that they covered charcoal, made from the stacked wood. He would like to come back and see a firing – when charcoal heated the hump so much that the new dishes in it went hard and glossy.

Buckhorn thought he and Travers would make camp outdoors as they usually did, but the pot people seemed to be having some sort of open visit. After Travers stated his purpose, (straightening himself up tall for once), the young woman at the door invited them in – both of them. They gave names all around and clasped hands. Otherwise they seemed off-guard and easy. The potter man was Mr. Lincoln, and the two potter women were his daughters. The woman at the door was his daughter also, but she was the oldest and seemed to be the woman of the house. Her name was Cinda. All of them were very pale. They were thin but not like Travers, and they all had hair the color of wet ashes. Cinda invited them to wash their hands and sit at table, where there was plenty of corncake, shared from a large dish at the center. Buckhorn felt at ease but on alert. There were three other men at the table. They were not pale, and he guessed they were visitors, perhaps come to buy pots too. They were a little older than he, but only one was fully grown. They called him Jackson, and the other two had names that sounded like Jackson. They looked to be brothers. All three stared at Buckhorn, and not at Travers, as they started to eat. "Trouble," he thought.

As Buckhorn returned their gaze, he sensed there was something familiar about them. The way they dressed, even the colors they wore, were not like the Lincolns. They were a little like – no, it wouldn't be. When they asked him where he lived (without saying a word to Travers) and he told them, the tension ended. "Boyo, we got us some Saponi in us, too. Never been to your High Ground, though."

Buckhorn looked proud. "You'd be welcome there. All you," as he looked around the table. Instantly, Jackson and Cinda exchanged glances, so briefly that Buckhorn almost missed it. He guessed the brothers were not here to buy pots.

Travers did not like the attention his "Neech" was getting. "Ma'am, this is the finest and dandiest corncake I have had. You must have grown the corn and had it ground nearby."

"Thank you, Mr. Travers, it is freshly ground, but I bought it from the miller. We take him dishes from time to time, and he sells them to people who come to the mill. A mill is as good as a store for buying things, don't you think? And far safer than merchants that have lawyers working for them nowadays, taking people to court for not paying their accounts before the regular year's-end. Maybe, Mr. Travers, it's the store-keepers who now work for the lawyers."

"Yes, Ma'am." That was the end of Travers's store of polite conversation. Buckhorn grinned. Miss Lincoln did not know how close to Travers's own actions her words had come.

Mr. Lincoln broke the silence. "How many jugs will you be wanting tomorrow? You'll be staying the night with us, of course."

"'Preciate it, Lincoln, surely I do. I'll want all the jugs I can lace onto my four horses, leaving enough room for the boy and me to ride. I traded a good store of skins for some of Tomm Toliver's whiskey, and I aim to fill up tomorrow and take it to Osborne's."

"A good plan," the potter nodded. "It's a pretty fair road beyond Toliver's. Your beasts should do well."

"Well, don't that suit all?" The brothers were back in the talk. "We have four casks of spruce beer our Pa just finished, and we're to take it to the Red Dog. Mind if we meet you here on the morrow, all loaded up, and we make a pack line together?"

Buckhorn was glad to hear that! Travers probably would not like the notion, but he could hardly refuse a sensible offer. This easily was the best day he had spent paying off what his people owned Snake Travers. The brothers went home soon. The girls banked up the fire and put down quilts by the hearth for Buckhorn and Travers. Turning his thankful heart to the Creator before falling asleep, Buckhorn asked himself what thing in this day had brought him most joy. The girl at Toliver's came first to mind, but then the brothers claiming "some Saponi" in their blood pushed her to second place.

Just before light, Travers waked him and they went to the pottery shed with the help of a pine torch Mr. Lincoln carried. Travers had plenty of deerskin strips for tying and lacing the empty jugs on the horses' backs and upper flanks. Buckhorn was not surprised that the brothers came early also, but he was not expecting their sister. She alit from the horse like a fiery dart, leaving the smallest brother on the blanket they had shared, and ran into the house. He could see she was clothed much like the boys, all of them wearing layers of skins against the cold. Two of their horses bore crossed wooden frames to support the casks and keep them secure, each animal carrying a cask on either side. Jackson and the next brother (Buckhorn thought it was Claxton) had a horse apiece with full saddlebags but no casks. They had five horses to add to Travers's four. Buckhorn wondered about the two horses he and Travers would ride. If would strain the animals if the trader filled all the jugs.

Inside, the girls had breakfast ready. Buckhorn and Travers were benefitting from sweetheart hospitality directed toward the brothers. He was sure now that Max was youngest and Clax was in the middle. Their people's name was Morgin. He saw no function for the Morgin girl except to enjoy the day and the people around her, and she was doing that.

Young Squire Needham

While Buckhorn and the others ate, Cinda answered a rap on the door, and a fine-looking white man entered. His heavy split-tailed coat was worn but clean and well-fitting. When he handed it to the woman, Buck saw parts of two shirts: a linen one next to the man's body that looked softened by many washings, and a full hunting shirt of thick wool woven with nettles. The man responded with a broad smile when Lincoln exclaimed,

"Squire Needham! Sit down with us and eat some of this food. My girls have over-cooked this morning, even for two bench-loads of men. You know the Morgin boys. Travers here is a skin trader. Travers and the man nodded.

"About time I got here to settle up with ye all for last year, Whitby. Weather delayed me getting back from the Halifax court, and I found my daughter sickly when I got home. Mrs. Needham is out of your yarbs she puts in poultices, too."

Buckhorn was surprised to hear the Morgin girl speak. "I thought Mrs. Needham grew yarbs, Sir."

"Oh yes, but she never had any luck growing rue and hyssop, says Whitby Lincoln's got the secret of them."

"Not many people who buy pots leave without some yarbs too." This time it was the middle Lincoln girl talking. "Most things Father gets from the woods, but he keeps his seeds from year to year from what his grandmother brought from England, things that don't grow wild here."

Buckhorn's people used plants to treat illness, and he wanted to know more. "What do you use against dip – dip-thery?"

No one spoke at first. Then the Morgin girl said, "That's a hard one. I heered of drying and grinding things that might help and then making a strong tea to drink from it. Walnut hulls, salt, agrimony, raspberry leaves, golden seal, and of course mullein – good old mullein."

Lincoln added, "I heered tell of a bark from the far side of Africa being good against diphtheria, but I've never known of any here. Greenheart, I think. Has there been diphtheria among your people?" he questioned Buckhorn.

"Not in my lifetime, but the elders fear it much."

"Where do you live, Boy?" the squire asked, looking straight Buckhorn for the first time.

"My home is called the High Ground in your speech, north of what is called Pine Ford in Orange County." Buckhorn was glad he had ventured into the Hillsborough court by curiosity once and knew these names. "My name is Buckhorn, Sir."

"Buck Corn," Needham repeated. "A strong name."

Buckhorn had not thought about Englishmen valuing the strength of names as his people did, and he wondered about the nature of this man Needham.

As they started the pack line, he noticed that Needham had come in an empty wagon. He must live where he can get here without a hard crossing. "Mr. Needham brought a wagon. Does that mean he will buy pots today?" he asked Clax Morgin.

"Likely. He keeps some stores to sell on his plantations, in easy reach of folks nearby. Salt, dirt dishes, plain chairs and benches, to-bac, sometimes cloth, remedies his wife makes up as salves and powders, what-not. We take him honey and spruce beer from time to time."

"What nature of man is he? Mr. Lincoln seems to respect him." Buckhorn was not sure he asked the question well.

"He seems honest for a big man in these parts. His Pa and uncle came in here early and got land when it was easy. His Pa has the same name, Brant Needham, and they're both 'justices' in the county court now, like all the big men are. I never heerd anything against Young Squire Needham, though, like using the court to squeeze and cheat folks. Allus treats us fair about trading, so far anyway."

Satisfied with Clax's answer, Buckhorn put his whole mind on watching about the pack line. The horses crossed the easy streams without a flicker, but when they got to wider water, he found out what the Morgin girl was good for. She and Max rode near the front. She alit near the water, reached in a saddle duffle, and pulled the biggest boots Buckhorn ever saw. She removed some of her leggings, pulled on the boots, and strapped the leggings above them, closing the boots tight. Into the water she splashed, holding the lead horse and the one behind it. The rest of the horses were being untied so that two would go across at a time. Buckhorn could see that the Morgin's horses were paired for this. The four horses he and Travers handled were less experienced. The girl stayed in the water for all the horses, even Travers's, coaxing, pushing, leaning on them just so. Jax stood on the far bank to pull them up. At first he seemed about to help her, but then he just looked on and did his part. Travers's four horses were last, and they were skittish when the empty jugs started shifting, but they did all right. She made Jax rest the horses a little after the crossing and went around to each horse and stroked them the way Buckhorn had seen some women of his people do. There were two more crossings like that one before they reached Toliver's.

A Surprise Visit

After making dough and milking, Lizzy spent most of the morning getting ready to make paper. 'Ro quickly grasped how to make the frame and set in the horsehairs crosswise like a tight strainer. He had wondered what use Mrs. Goody would find for all the hair from horses' tails she had made him save and hang on pegs in the stable. He was eager to see how Miss Lizzy was going to make paper, though. Lizzy got all the worn-out linen she could find, some of it old and dirty, of course, but she boiled it outside. It was not a regular washing, with 'Ro hauling a lot of water, but he did haul some. She built the fire herself after straining the milk, so the water was almost boiling when she put in the old cloth and banked up some of the coals to keep the heat even. She had to go inside for kitchen work and leave the pot unattended. That was not a good thing to do. Also, she wished she could stay outside and be sure to see Buckhorn. Travers likely would come for his whiskey today, and the boy was her first recruit to help her find Davo.

There was too much going on inside. Goody barked orders as soon as Lizzy got in, all having to do with getting a big dinner ready for noon with enough left to be added to when they served supper. Not unusual, but Lizzy's time out for paper preparations had set Goody back, and Goody did not like to hustle all that much. Lizzy worked automatically, and time fled. The minute she toted the last of the dinner into the tavern, she whipped outside to check the boiling pot, afraid it had boiled too high, lost water, and scorched the precious old rotted linen.

"Calm yourself," she thought, as she saw the pot. "Goody has taken pity and gone to check." As she moved closer to the sitting, stirring figure she saw it was not Goody. It was . . . Ruly? Ruly Morgin?

"What, where?" Lizzy stammered, looking at Ruly like she was a ghost.

Ruly smirked. "Gone off to leave the washing, have you? What a no-account apprentice! And what kind of nastiness is in that pot? You people don't wear the likes of that, surely. You need some clean animal skins to wear, you do now." Ruly laughed and threw open her arm to hug Lizzy. They jumped up and down in the hug.

"I am so glad to see you. I can't believe . . . where did you come from?"

"I didn't tell you that day at court, because I was afeared Tomm Toliver would not get you, but I live not too far from here. My brothers are in the Red Dog now, delivering spruce beer. They come here from time to time, but they never let me come. I made them bring me today. I wanted to surprise my friend, Miss O'Canning. Then I found her washing about to boil out."

They sat on the ground in the sun and yammered like magpies from the same nest. Ruly was amazed that Lizzy was about to make paper and told her she would help get the linen out. She wanted to know all about what Lizzy had to do for Goody and was not surprised by the work load. She was surprised when Lizzy told her Goody was not awful and could be kind and funny. That was not a Goody Ruly had ever heard about.

"She benefits from getting used to," Lizzy explained. "I do have enough to eat, and I sleep warm and am not fearful for my safety."

"That's important. You'll be showing womanhood soon, and keeping safe is hard on your own. I say that, and my two older brothers breathe over me like I'm a perishing rosebud. That's why they won't let me go with them into a public house. I promised them I would not go inside the Red Dog today, that I just wanted a visit with you. If you're going to be working more in the Red Dog, maybe they'll bear for me to go in with them. Surely. Zeus, Lizzy, you'll catch a beau in the Red Dog, with all the young bucks that do come and go there."

Lizzy did not want a buck nor a beau now. She might want a beau in a few years, though. She said nothing in response.

Ruly peered at her solemnly before speaking. "Have you had your first mense?"

"Mints?" Why was Ruly talking about butter-cream sweets?

"My aunt on Deep River gave me some mints when we were there some years ago."

"No, silly. I mean the blood that comes to a growing-up girl every month, down between the legs, in the private parts. Has your monthly bleeding started?"

Now Lizzy was embarrassed. "Mother told me about that after she sickened. I guess she thought she might not be alive when it came. I did not pay much attention. It seemed a far-off unimportant thing then. Does it hurt? How do you know when it's about to come?"

"It doesn't feel like you're cut and bleeding, nothing like that. My aunt told me the blood is not regular blood but is a cushion where a baby would grow if a woman has one a-building inside her. When a month or so goes by and there is no baby started, the cushion turns loose and falls out a little at a time over several days. Then a new one grows. If there is a baby started, the cushion stays in place and makes a nice spot for the baby to grow and gets nourishment to the baby. A woman getting her mense every month brings to my mind the moon times for planting and such like." Ruly pretended to fan her face, sighing "A woman shares her secret only with the moon."

"You really do know a lot. Has yours started?" Lizzy figured it had.

"Aye. You'll want to keep out some of those pieces of linen. I fasten strips next to my body to take up the bleeding. It's not a bad job to wash out the strips and dry them. A lot easier than a baby's diaper! Not the same thing at all; the mense is fresh clean blood. While there's a flow, I wash out the used strip every time I put on a fresh one. The blood comes right out. Just be sure to use cold water. Hot water will set the blood, just like any kind of blood."

Lizzy already knew blood needed cold water to get it out, so this part was not news.

"I wonder what women do who don't have cloth."

"I have heered of women using clean moss, just placing it in their clothes or tying it to theirselves with leather strips. Then they throwed it in a stream. Easy enough, I say."

"I am definitely keeping back some of this boilt linen for myself." Then added, "Do you have enough? There are old sheets and rags in a public house."

"You are a kind person, Lizz-O. I don't need any now, but thank you for the future. Now let's take all this linen down to the creek and rinse it out."

"I have a big clean sunny place picked out near the creek where we can lay it out to dry. The sun will bleach it even more."

While they worked the linen, Lizzy told Ruly she wanted to find Davo and for Ruly to keep her ears open, especially if she went to the next court.

Changes

Lizzy got into the tavern business in earnest. Tomm found an old ledger book with only a few pages used. He tore them out and saved them in a clean wooden box for the next time Lizzy and 'Ro made paper. They had set up the presses in a kitchen corner, out of the way of the cutting and cooking places. The fire kept the air dry, even in their "paper corner" across the room. It took about five days to get the first sheets dry and crisp, and after that, they kept the frames filled so that a supply of paper was steady. Lizzy cut the first sheet into small squares, "chits" she called them, and sewed bunches of them together at one corner, using a needle and a stingy amount of thread. She cut the other first sheets into pages and sewed them together properly at one side and called that a "daybook." She kept making chits and daybooks as new sheets dried.

At first, Lizzy was the only one to write on the chits, but Tomm and Goody joined in after two busy nights. They wrote each customer's name at the top of a chit and wrote what they served that customer for one day only. They kept the corner-sewn bunch of chits behind the counter and flipped to a man's chit to record each tankard, beer pot, dram, cup, pipe of tobacco, trencher, and dish. This was good for Lizzy's goal of finding about Davo, because it made her learn the men's names and a little of their manner. The buyer saw when she wrote on his chit. When he was ready to leave, Lizzy quickly totaled his chit for that day, and he either paid or added the amount to his credit. Lizzy's speed with figures made this easy. This was exactly what Tomm and Goody had been doing all along, except they had not written any of it down until the customer was ready to leave, and memory could be slippery. After a few nights, the Tolivers could see that they were taking in more money (and recording more credit) than they used to do.

After the tavern emptied at night, or no later than first thing the next morning, one of them, (Lizzy at first), transferred what each customer bought onto the daybook, one page for each day. As she recorded each transaction into the daybook, she struck through the chit record. After both sides of a chit had been recorded and struck through, the used chit went into the box for making new paper. It took about a month to fill a daybook;. Then it was time to transfer the daybook records to the ledger where each customer had his "debit" and "credit" page. In the ledger, the customers were in more-or-less alphabetical order, so it was easy to find a person's page when copying from the daybook to the ledger. When a ledger was up-to-date, every customer could see instantly how much he owned or if anything were owned him, just as people did in stores, mills, and other trading places. Lizzy told Tomm it was not necessary to record the rare cash transactions in the daybooks, since they did not affect the ledger, unless he just wanted to keep up with how much of everything he was selling. Tomm said he wouldn't go that far down the ciphering trail and what Lizzy had them doing was fine enough. The whole changeover from the old way to the new way went far easier than Lizzy had expected! She was glad they believed her when she first told them the Red Dog would take in more profit this way. And it did. Even the dog on the sign seemed pleased when Tomm gave it a new coat of bright red paint.

The work in the tavern tired Lizzy more than cleaning and cooking did, and that surprised her. She thought it was because she was having to learn new names and faces at the same time she was showing the Tolivers how to keep their accounts. After they were used to it, Goody took to keeping the daybook and ledger, the "paperwork," she called it. Lizzy was glad. She found she was eating more now, and growing. The few shifts and skirts she owned got too short, and the armholes of the shifts began to pinch. She made do with her own alterations, even sewing a straight band of old woolen goods along the bottoms of her skirts for a proper length, and it looked ugly. The time came when Goody had to give her some cloth. Lizzy made a skirt from two of Goody's old woolen ones. Goody gave her two old sheets that Lizzy thought would be better used for paper, but at least the shifts Lizzy made from them fit well and were soft. She added tucks in the wide straps and in the skirt so they could be let out, the way her mother had done when she was little. Aprons were easy. Any old things could be pieced together for apron cloth. Lizzy thought it a good thing there were no looking glasses about to see how her clothes looked on her. When she caught her image over a bowl of water, she saw that her face and hair had become softer and livelier, and that pleased her. But the whole image – it must be dismal.

Something about her was getting clumsy. She would feel chirpy for a while and then really droopy. She never slept long enough. When she felt bad, she resented her work more than ever, even with Goody seeming to think more of her than at first. Her arms and legs seemed strangely long, and she dropped things! Oh, did she drop things. And she stumbled. She overheard Goody telling Tomm that "the gull" was falling over her own feet and asking if she were "imbibing" behind the counter. Lizzy thought that meant drinking something that would make her stupid or drunk, and she surely was not. It made her nervous when Goody seemed to be watching her so. The mad old biddy! Painted up like a peacock, mean as a crow, and with the brain of grass-hopping sparrow. Once Lizzy broke three bowls in three days, toting food to the tavern. She did not slip or trip. It was not raining. She did not know why she dropped them. They just slipped through her hands while she walked. The same dishes she had carried before, filled with the same food. Goody lit into her the second time and turned downright heathen the third time. It made Lizzy so mad she cried. She bawled. She didn't know why, if it was because Goody was so mean, or because Lizzy hated breaking the dishes. She had not meant to. Life was getting ugly. She thought back on Mother and tried harder not to think down-mouth thoughts, but that advice, and that person, seemed so far away they were not real anymore. That made her cry harder.

Scaldhead!

When Lizzy had her downward feelings, the hope of learning something about Davo got her focused, time after time. She was in the Red Dog every day now and knew most of the people who came in. She had confided to a few of the customers, starting with Young Squire Needham. Ruly had told her she had heard he was a good man and knew everybody. It was hard to speak to him at first, but once she saw him by himself, she took her pitcher over to him and made herself tell him who she was and that she was worried about Davo. He said he remembered the giving out of apprentices and was glad Tomm took her. He remembered that the man Leetch had taken Davo, but he did not say one way or the other about Leetch. He could see the girl was near tears when she said David was not yet ten. Lizzy wanted to think he would remember about Davo when he next went near Leetch's shop. She did not expect a promise, and he gave none.

She talked also with Mr. Marshall, the man who sometimes read a newspaper aloud to anyone who wanted to hear. She had listened the night he talked about a vestry law, and he seemed to know what all was going on. He was not a regular customer, so she made sure to speak to him the first time she saw him again. It seemed easier, now that she had spoken to the squire. Mr. Marshall did not live in Johnston County and had not heard of Leetch, but he said he would ask around. He wanted to know where she had aunts or uncles and how she was getting along without her family.

"I'll pray for you and your brother, Child, and that is no hollow talk. One of the things about praying is that it reminds us to do what we can about what we're praying for. Some say we're putting in the Creator's hands, but I believe He can use our feet, so to speak. Besides, it's already in the Creator's hands, and He won't let me forget about you and David."

The more men she talked to, the more worried she became. The ones who had heard of Leetch either did not like him themselves or had heard bad things about him. The talk was that at least one apprentice had died there, but nobody could say what happened. She told Tomm about it, hoping he would at least tell her how to get to Leetch's and give her a day or two off and the use of Snap to go see for herself. He shook his head and looked sorrowful. "'Tis a pity, Gull, 'tis indeed, there be men who don't take proper care of 'prentices like Goody does." That sounded like Tomm was washing Lizzy's troubles away from his own hands.

Late one afternoon, two of Ruly's brothers and Pa Morgin came in. Lizzy recognized the boys but did not know their names. They had been hunting all day and brought in dressed rabbits and a porcupine skin for trade. Tomm and Lizzy were glad to see the quills, and Lizzy took it all to the kitchen. Rabbit stew tomorrow. Hurrying back, she served them. After they started tucking in to their supper, it seemed a good time to introduce herself.

"We know you. Ruly told us. Don't you fillies go getting in trouble together. That's all our sister's good for." That was the younger one, but his brother kicked him under the bench.

"Shet yo' gob, Clax. You jest wish you could handle horses like she can."

"Please, would you tell Ruly I have learned nothing yet about my brother. She'll understand."

"Well, give us to understand your meaning, Missy." Pa's look was either interested or displeased; Lizzy couldn't tell which. Briefly she told them about Davo.

The older brother interrupted her. "I remember the boy from court. Feisty-looking little pine knot. Mayhap Leetch will try to break his spirit."

"Aw, Jax, you ain't the only one seed him. Looked like a speck o' rosin to me."

"Enough, boys," their pa said. "Clax, you got too much mouth on you." Turning to Lizzy, he dismissed her with, "We'll tell Ruly we seed you. Ye'd be welcome to visit if ye get a chance."

Mr. Marshall was a surprise when he showed up sooner than Lizzy expected. He sought her out right away, wearing a troubled look.

"I've no good news for you, but I do know the boy is sick." I went to Leetch's and said I was a friend of David O'Canning's family and wished to give word from his sister. Leetch would not let me pass, saying the boy was phlegmy. I went straightway to the nearest justice of the peace, Squire Crenshaw, expecting him to give me or his constable a paper to require Leetch to let me see the boy. I have done similar things before, and I doubted not of the outcome." He paused for breath, and Lizzy leaned forward.

"Crenshaw refused to do anything! Said Leetch was in his rights and that he, Crenshaw, had seen the boy last week and there was nothing amiss. I went to one of Crenshaw's neighbors, a respectable man I know, and he went with me back to Crenshaw. The rascal cursed us, and him a magistrate! He threatened to call his constable on me and take me to the sheriff's house for lock-up." Lifting his pot of spruce beer, Marshall swallowed twice, set down the pot, and looked at Lizzy.

"I do not know whether your brother is seriously ill or not, but something is wrong, and Crenshaw knows it. On my way here, I went to another magistrate, but he was not at home. We can find a magistrate to intervene, but if the boy is ill he needs help now."

"It must not be a phlegm, Sir. The master would have him up and working with a phlegm, unless it had turned into something worse."

"I went on to Osborne's and axed about, quiet-like, if there was any sickness. Always there is in early spring, and a traveler would enquire. The usual ague and catarrh in the throat, some fevers, nothing out of the ordinary. One man thought back to early fall and said there had been several cases of scald-head."

"But David was not there until January."

"I know. The condition is rare in winter. But if the worm that causes it is living in a protected place, like a building, it can survive until it finds a host. Such worms have been known to stay alive in places that don't get much cleaning. The apprentice room in Leetch's shop could be such a place. My opinion is that your brother may well have scald head from the fall infestation, since there is no generalized sickness about the place."

"I saw people with scald-head and heered the use of medicinal for it, but what happens if it is not treated? Will the worm keep eating away at the person's scalp?" Lizzy was trembling.

"Most people recover, but some die, particularly if the body is weak, like an old person or a malnourished child." Lizzy did not doubt that Davo was malnourished, from what she had heard of Leetch. Davo could die!"

Thinking aloud, she tried to make a plan. "I will need the proper medicinal, and I will have to get Goody to let me take time off and go. Where will I find the right medicinal? The potter has some medicinals, and Squire Needham's wife has some. But what medicinal is good for scald-head?"

"I am sorry I know little of these things. I do carry a book with a few remedies." Quickly he went to the stable and brought back a small book from his saddlebag. "It says bloodroot and celandine will kill the tetter worm. I do not know it myself. Once the worm is dead and removed, or all the worms if there are more, the healing salves people commonly make will help the skin heal. Lizzy, I will spend the night here and go out again to find a magistrate who will help. I will tell Mrs.

Toliver directly that your brother's life may be at stake. Surely, she will let you have time to go to him and return. How long have you been at the Red Dog?"

"Not four months yet, Sir."

"She still ought to let you go. No use talking with Tomm Toliver. He only gives in to her, blinded as he is. Is there someone who could go with you?"

Ruly jumped into her mind. "I think so."

"Then, the first thing you need to know is where to get celandine and how to fetch it. All the root people will have bloodroot. I do not know this neighborhood well. You will have to find out from other visitors."

Suddenly, Lizzy remembered her manners and saw the great trouble Mr. Marshall had gone to. "Please, Sir, I thank you with all my heart. I do truly."

"I know you do, Lizzy. I know you do. We must act."

No one in the tavern knew where to get celandine. They suggested the people Lizzy already knew about but could not say if they had celandine. She ran toward the kitchen, hoping 'Ro was there, and when he was not, she ran to his stable and beat on the door.

He answered the door, boots in hand, for he was cleaning them. "Miss Lizzy?"

Before he could ask, she blurted out her need. "Does the woman Minerva at Mrs. McBee's have more than the common sorts of medicinal? I heered she is a Wise Woman. Mighten she have celandine?" She did not need to explain how she knew his familiarity with the family.

"Might be, might be. If anybody does, she does. That scald-head bad. I seed a girl had lost all the hair and skin on her head, and half her face and neck-skin was rotted." His brow furrowed tight, then he said, "Mr. Tomm and Mrs. Goody not gone let me go up there in the night-time. I know that. I just take Snap and fly up there and fly right back by daybreak. Miz Minerva give me something! She sure to." Wa'ro pulled on his boots.

"I'll find a way to pay her, Wa'ro."

A lone sweet potato remained on his platter. Tucking it in his pocket, he handed the patter to Lizzy, grabbed his wrap from the wall, and ran to get Snap. Lizzy remembered to move his warming rock from the kitchen to the stable.

The Plan

Wa'ro hoped to get to the McBee place before midnight. They would be sound asleep, likely. He would wake Ahmee first. He chuckled to think how that would surprise her. He never went anywhere near her bed when he visited. They sat up by the low fire together while Minerva, Gaspar, and Ahmee's brother slept. He was almost one of the family, and what a family it was. He wanted one like it, except *free.* Could not get those thoughts out of his mind. Nor did he want to.

The moon looked small and far away when he got there. It was easier than he thought to creep into the quarter. Ahmee's family was the only one with a whole house. Soon he was standing behind Ahmee as she entered her parents' room and shushed them awake. Quickly, Wa'ro stated his need, and Minerva was standing up by the time he finished, wrapping herself. Her husband sat up, but she whispered, "No trouble. It's a medicine need. Don't rouse yourself."

"Can you tell me how bad the boy's tetter is, how long he's had it, or anything?"

"No'm. Not even sure it be tetter, but they think it be. Miss Lizzy say she need celandine and bloodroot. Any advice from you too, she want. She say she find a way to pay you."

"Uuummh. No matter. You know that. She needs some barberry, too. I'm putting all three powders in this box. Tell her to save some back for if she needs more and to boil three eggshells of the powder with a goodly mug of sweet milk and put it in a bottle with a lid, for carrying. It will keep fresh till it is used up. You remember all this for her, Wa'ro. She needs to wash all the afflicted place with clean water and good soap. Air it dry, then dab the poultice all over the places. It will drip a little, and it won't set up much. She needs to put a clean, light piece of linen loosely over his head and wherever. This needs painting twice in the morning, then mid-afternoon and bedtime. Four times. Every day till it's used. I'm sending some healing salve, too, but don't use it until the poultice treatment is over. The poultice will kill the worm if it's used right. Then the salve will help the places heal up."

"You call it a poultice. Will it get dry or hard?"

"No. I told you, it won't set up much. How old is the boy, and do you know his nature?"

"Near about ten years. I know nothing except what his sister say, that he be little for his age, brave, and he works for a mean man who has a name for not feeding his help like he ought. He added, "His sister is my friend. That is why I am asking you for this. I came away without Mr. Tomm knowing."

Minerva glanced at Ahmee. "Then get on your way and be sharp. I hope Sister will be a friend to you when you need her." Minerva's neck tightened as she said that.

Thanking Minerva, he walked outside with Ahmee.

"I hope this chance-taking is worth it, Wa'ro. If the boy lives on account of you, that Miss Lizzy is going to be surely in your debt. You think on that."

"I am thinking on that, but that's not what-for I'm helping her." He hugged her hard and led Snap toward the road.

When Lizzy went out to milk next morning, Wa'ro was out and stirring as usual. He gave her the medicines and instructions in the cow byre, where it was not unusual for them to talk. How would she get to Davo? Mr. Marshall had told her how to get to the shop and where there was a little window on the room Davo likely stayed. Leetch lived in a house nearby. Had the preacher had any luck with Goody? Something told her to speak to Tomm first.

"No, Gull. Don't ill Goody. Mad as a settin' hen she was last night after Marshall told her ye ought to have time and a horse to go to yer brother. 'Twill be good now if she quits carrying on about "what a proper gennilman Mr. Marshall be."

"But. . .?" Lizzy hated it when her lower lip trembled.

"Quiet, now, Gull. Yer Tomm's got a plan. You need Miss Rhulia to go with you. She's just the one, and she has a horse faster'n Snap. I'll go to her, and I know she'll come. I'll give her pa some line of talk if he be troublesome, say it's women's business. You can see for yourself if the boy's bad sick, and just in case, take some of Goody's sorrel vinegar in a flask to clean out whatever's got a holt on him. Allus good for itches and such."

Tomm had no idea she already had medicines, and the sorrel vinegar would be wonderful. "Thank you. You are a kind man. But what will Goody. . .?"

He laughed. I'll tell her I need more platters from Lincoln, now that ye've about broke us up, and I'll go on to Morgins." No longer jolly, he added, "Ye likely wonder why I don't stand up to the cuss and tell 'er what's what." Lizzy did wonder but said nothing.

"I live with her every day. She's proud in her heart that she's crowed against the preacher and got her way. She'll play Lady Gracious with me and all o'us till that wears off. You be set to go before supper, and I'll dismiss you early tonight. Cover ye straw, and leave in a roundabout way. It's a good road most of the way."

Lizzy beamed. "You're no idjit, Sir, that's for sure."

For most of the day, she kept a list in her head of what she needed for the trip and gathered it up, using a tall empty cabinet to hide it. As soon as Ruly got there, she filled her saddlebags with all Lizzy had gathered. Lizzy even had a haunch of roast pork wrapped in clean shucks and a bottle of broth for her brother. Ruly herself could not have thought up such a fine escapade! They made sure to fill their own bellies from Goody's cook-pot before they left.

There was no trouble getting there. The biggest stream was the one near the Red Dog. They kept quiet the whole way and twice pulled over into the woods when they sensed other people on the road. Copper, Ruly's stallion, was fast. The night was bracing but not keen, and here and there, freshly-turned earth added its scent to the girls' anticipation. Marshall had said the dwelling house was on the far side of the shop from the room where he thought David was. They tied Copper in the woods and carried the saddlebags to the likely window, stepping like moths.

The Intervention

David was in a dirty, clogged river. He could see himself drowning like his pa, but this was not a freshet. Nasty smells burned his nose. Colored lights and sparking blobs changed shapes, going in, out, around, back together, faster than white clouds ever did when he lay and watched them at Mother's. Was he asleep? Was he dead and not yet in Heaven or Hell? It might be the way to Hell, but it was better than living at the place he had to be. He could not think. His mind flashed off like the colored lights. Now some of the lights were black. How could that be? Too hard to think. Now floating again. That was better. No more thrashing. Easy.

Bodies next to him, rubbing, hurting him. His head had come off his body already, and the demons were digging where his head used to be. He could not stop them, so he faded away again. "Drink, David." How did they know his name? One felt like Mother. Mayhap he was in Heaven with her, but why did he hurt in Heaven? Something in his mouth was good, good. He tried to swallow. More came. Then wet cloths in this pukey river. Why? He quit. It all quit.

The candle stubs were mostly used up after they had worked on Davo about two hours. Lizzy had never imagined such stench, filth, and putrid flesh. How long had he been like this? The rubbing on his sores did not wake him, but it did make him squirm and flail weakly. Maybe it was good he was not awake, for this must be paining him awful. The girls took turns holding him down and working on his sores. The one holding him put her body next to him to try to warm him. There was no heat in the room. The whole scalp was a run-together blister, or so it looked. There were places where something had burst where he had tossed on the bed and then scabbed over. Ruly disappeared and returned with sticks of pine lighter'd from some chunks she had spotted in the woods. Once they had cleaned all they could get to while Davo was on his back and sides and painted Minerva' poultice, they pulled out what cloth there was on the shuck bed and put down a clean sheet Lizzy had packed. Then they put a smaller cloth under his back and head, turned him over, and finished their cleaning. Finally they removed the small cloth, and the sick boy at least was cleaned up. He swallowed some broth from time to time but was far from   awake.

Ruly and Lizzy lay on either side of him now, wrapping them with their arms and with a bed rug that had slipped off earlier and escaped getting nasty. They lay still, hoping Davo was getting good rest now. There were only a few hours of darkness left, and the man Leetch and whoever else lived here would be up and about. Lizzy's mind ran to what could happen next. She could not leave Davo as he was. If miraculously he awoke, talked and could understand her, she could tell him what to do with the poultice and salves, and the girls might make it back before Goody could know. Lizzy could not help but play that out in her mind, but she had to think about what was more likely. Ruly could go back to the Red Dog and give a full account. Lizzy had confidence in Mr. Marshall; sooner or later, a JP or constable would get here and look into Leetch's treatment of Davo. Something awful was liable to happen to her, no matter what. Would Goody throw her back to the court where she would get a truly awful master? Goody and Tomm could do that. Now that Lizzy had trained them in keeping their records, they had the best she could give them. Wa'ro knew how to make paper, and they could get another apprentice to be Goody's   workhorse.

Something worse than Goody's anger waited for Lizzy. There was no telling what Leetch would do. He would have no trouble getting Squire Crenshaw to take her to the sheriff. Then the sheriff would take her to court to be punished. It might turn into a big blowup all over the county. Nothing in her life might ever be the same. No doubt, it would come out that Wa'ro had slipped out at night, and with Tomm's horse! She was sure the court would punish that. At least a lashing. Would Tomm sell him as a message to other slaves? Not on his own, Tomm wouldn't, but if the big men told him to, what would he do? Tomm could not operate a tavern without a license from the county.

Whatever Pandora's box Lizzy would open by staying to take care of Davo, she knew she would do it. If she left him like this, he likely would die. She was not able to get past that hard truth.

She'd better tell Ruly she was staying so Ruly could decide what to do before light. She whispered across Davo's head, "Ruly, I am going to stay. If you go now, you can get to the Red Dog before Goody sees I'm gone. It will make it easier on Tomm, and he has been good to me, especially about this."

Ruly was asleep, though! How in the world could a body sleep with all they were facing? Lizzy felt another tinge of wishing she could be more like Ruly. After a time, Ruly stirred and sat up. Both of them needed to go outside and relieve themselves, so they took turns, Ruly going first. When she came back, Lizzy said what she needed to say.

"Lizzy-o, you proper little numskull! I'll not leave. Here, you put this in a pocket under your apron. Practice opening it first, so you can be quick. If you have to use it, don't slide it like a fingernail. Plunge it straight in, up to here. If you still need it, do it again in another hole." It was a folding horn knife. Lizzy shuttered but practiced opening it. Then she slipped through the window and into the woods. While she was out, she found Copper's grain bag and fastened it on. No need to have the horse hungry and restless.

Back at the open window, she heard the door being unlocked and saw it open. She ducked and scurried to the stack of lighter'd, picking a good-sized piece for swinging, one with a knot near the big end.

Busted

Lizzy saw the door creak open and a woman's elbow pry it open. She was holding a trencher with wet pone bread on it and spoke as she edged in. "Wal air ye daid yet, ye pile o'vermin?"

Ruly let the woman see her before she spoke. "He's near dead from neglect. We've come to take care of him, and I can see that means getting him away from Mr. Leetch till he's well." Ruly was standing tall and talking full-grown woman, a sight to see. Lizzy thought she remembered the woman from court, the one whose foot stank when she took off her shoe. Neither the woman nor Ruly could see Lizzy. Should Lizzy hit the woman with the lighter'd knot and hope to knock her out, then they could grab Davo, mattress and all, and get him up to Osborne's? Why had they not planned what to do if they got caught like this? Maybe they could talk the woman into letting them take Davo long enough to get him well? Was the woman a servant, or was she Leetch's wife? Probably his wife.

In the three or four seconds Lizzy was thinking what to do, the woman decided what to do, herself. Rather than take on Ruly alone, she screamed, "Rasco, quick! Robbers! Now!"

Ruly wheeled the woman around, holding her from behind, the open horn knife at her ribs. Ruly's feet were spread, and she clasped her chin tightly on the top of the woman's head. A lucky fit. The yellow streaks in Ruly's brown eyes seemed to shoot like stars.

Lizzy slipped just behind the edge of the open door. The woman didn't see her, but Lizzy thought Ruly did. Lizzy held her lighter'd knot over her head, ready for Leetch to come barreling through the door. When he did, she jumped straight up and used all her strength plus her extra height to wham the top of his head and send him a-winding. She thought it was a good strike. Sounded like wood cracking on wood.

The strike didn't do what Lizzy thought it would, though. The man fell, all right, like a tree, but he crashed into Ruly. On the way down, his wife twisted out of Ruly's hold and got away, just as Leetch gasped, "go get Hersch an' his boy!"

This was turning into a real fight! Lizzy kept banging the man's shoulders, because he and Ruly were knife-fighting hard and fast. What if he killed Ruly? Lizzy wanted to stop him from sinking his blade into her friend, just the way Ruly had showed Lizzy how to do. Lizzy kept on hammering away at his knife arm. Maybe she could get the knife away from him if she wore him down.

It was not to be. Two more men came running in and forced the girls off Leetch. Right away, Lizzy saw the older man was Squire Crenshaw, the one who had rushed the court to make Davo Leetch's apprentice, and who had refused to let Mr. Marshall see Davo.

"Wail," Crenshaw sneered, two feisty wenches a-try in' to rob their betters! Sheriff'll be glad to have you'uns as lock-ups in his barred basement till next court, and ye'll get enough charges to put you'uns out in sarvis till ye'r old, toothless, witches. Not that ye're any man's purty gals now."

"We didn't rob, Sir." Lizzy was trying to be polite. "That's my poor brother yonder, suffering something awful. We came in the night to tend him, to wash his blisters and put poultices. We put a clean sheet under him instead of the filthy rags he was laying in, and him unconscious."

Crenshaw cut her off. "Naw, Gal, this is about two nosy nellies breaking in a man's house an' interferon' in his conduct as a tradesman in charge of a pore orphan apprentice. And ye assaulted the woman of the house, just as she was comin' in to minister to the boy. Horseshoe, tie up these nellies, to tek 'em to the sheriff. I need me a place to write out yer affidavys, Leetch, to send Sheriff Night to hold them in arrest."

A big awkward boy-man grinned and started tying ropes on the girls' wrists. Lizzy wondered why he looked familiar, then remembered he was one of them she had seen fighting outside the courthouse that day. Ruly was sneering at him, so Lizzy figured her friend knew him.

Leetch, and then his wife, told their version of the girls' "breaking and entering" and their "assaults" and "trespassing," all of it "contrary to the peace of the colony of North Car'liny."

Crenshaw read it aloud as he wrote it down, changing some of what they said to the odd words Lizzy had heard in court. So, that will be the charges against Ruly and me, she realized -- not a word about poor Davo and why we came here!

With her hands tied behind her, she turned to Mrs. Leetch. "Please, Missus, I brought poultice for my brother. See, there is some on him already. He may live if you will be kind enough to treat his sores with the poultice four times a day and spoon him some broth. There is some by the bed. He'll be no good to you dead, and you can save his life. Please, Missus." Lizzy was begging, and Little Brother was well worth it.

"Come on, here, you skinny wench! Paw, can I tie 'em together and make 'em walk ahead o' me to Night's?"

"That's 'Sheriff Night,' boy. You're my constable, so be decent about it. Yes, they are to walk in front, but no whip, you hear? I don't aim to get my office questioned on account of yore ways."

Ruly spoke very calmly, even proudly: "We won't need to walk. We have a horse tied in the woods." She was not about to leave Copper!

"Stole 'im, I reckon," Crenshaw spat.

Ruly didn't bother to contradict him. Leetch by now had found Copper and brought him close.

"He is needing water now, if you please." She spoke in her calm way, eyes straight ahead, not looking at anybody.

With Copper watered, the girls got on his back, their hands still tied. Crenshaw's look lingered on Copper. His son already was mounted next to the girls, saying they had to stay just a little in front of him and "not be a-yammering on but be quiet, in respect of the law," for which he, "the constable of this district," was "a-tekken them in to meet justice."

"Hold on, there, boy. I aim to tek these heifers in. You can go along with us."

"Paw!" Horseshoe squealed. "This is MY detail. I'm the constable. You're jes the justice. You write the charges, and I tek the prisoners and the charges to the sheriff. Now, don' you go a-crowdin' me on my first duty."

While the boy whined, Herschel Crenshaw was adjusting himself in his own saddle and nudging Copper along. "Fine hoss, fine hoss," he laughed in Leetch's direction. "This case could be worth a trip and a little more fancying up of the charges."

The three horses rode most of the morning. They were retracing part of their journey up to Leetch's, so the way was not new to Lizzy. She had such wretched thoughts that she did not even notice the spring buds she could not see last night. She fought the worst of her thoughts, remembering that they had cleaned and treated Davo and that the fierce little fellow was still alive. Mrs. Leetch might even have the heart to treat him, if only to keep herself and Leetch from looking bad. Horseshoe rode close behind, sometimes beside them, and he wouldn't let them talk. The sun was nearly midpoint when they took a road toward the river and saw the outline of Snipes Night's compound.

Waking up in a Wagon

Davo was out of the murky river now. No more swirling lights or swooshing, churning water. He might even be able to push his eyes open, if he could just rest up some. He couldn't lay still to rest; there was swaying and bumping under him. It seemed like the muddy river had turned into a rocky road and he was fastened onto it. Could he even move? He pushed hard and thought he felt his foot move, then flexed his fingers and tried to move his head. No, no, his head was a big rock. Felt like hornets stinging all over his head. He got one eye to where he could see a little. He was lying in a wagon! Down, like a baby in a crib, in the floor of a wagon in a pile something -- straw, leaves, and some kind of coverlid. Where was that devil Leetch? Was he the one driving the wagon? Does he think I'm dead and carrying me to bury me?

Davo must have stirred, for the driver turned his head and looked down at him. He was a mystery to Davo, but he had a kind face.

"Well, Young Pup, ye've determined to live some more? A good thing, too! Ye've not lived in this world long enough to work for the air ye've breathed, nor the water that's dribbled down yer pipe!"

"Who are ye, Sir, and does my master know ye have me?" Davo was not sure all the words came out. He thought he liked this man, and anybody was better than Leetch, but what was happening? Davo tried to push himself up but fell back down in the straw. What had happened to him? His close-set eyes were pale and faint but full of question.

"Ye've been sick, Lad, powerful sick. Don't fret about Mr. Leetch for a while. I'm moving you to my house, where my good wife can feed you and take care of those sores. When you get well, the court can sort out where you'll stay." He added, so low the boy could barely hear, "but it won't be back to Rasco Leetch, if I'm alive."

It was coming to Davo that this man, whoever he was, had rescued him from the torments he had been through at the wagon maker's.

He remembered how his mother had taught him to talk to men he respected. "Please, Sir, how did you know I needed help?" He didn't remember ever seeing this man at Leetch's shop.

"Well, now, yer a lucky pup all right. That sister of yers has been asking everybody she sees if they know how yer faring in the wagon business. She heered round-about-like that Leetch has a name for not feeding his help enough. Me being a justice of the peace, she axed me to look about for you when I was in this neighborhood. So I did, and I didn't like what I seed."

"Lizzy! You know Lizzy! Where is she?"

"She lives at a public house south of here. She's apprenticed to the owners, name of Toliver. She works hard, and I think she's in a good place. She's smart, and folk there do like her."

The boy was smiling. It looked like it hurt him, with all the raw skin and dried poultice, but it was a smile all right. The man didn't want to tell him where Lizzy was now and that she was in trouble. He did want to tell him how Lizzy had come in the night and cleaned up his sores, but that would have to wait.

"We'll get you well, David O'Canning, and there'll be time to decide who you can live with and work for. We're done talking, now, you start your rest-up, so ye'll be fit to work!"

Davo decided right then that he would work hard at anything this man needed done. Whoever he was.

The Man in the Wagon Seat

Brant Needham, Jr. thought on what he had done this morning, using his JP authority to check on the boy. It was true, a complaint had come to him, from no less respected a man than Elder Marshall. Leetch had not let Marshall see the sick boy. That was enough for Needham to make a warrant to force Leetch to show the boy. Needham knew it was pure luck that Herschel Crenshaw had not been home. Being the nearest justice, Crenshaw would have challenged Needham, and unlike Needham, Crenshaw had a constable at hand, even if it was that otherwise worthless Horseshoe. Why would a man call his son "Horseshoe"? No wonder the boy could not feel sure of himself. Some folks knew his real name was Herschel, Jr. Others likely just thought his ma and pa were weak-minded. Squire Crenshaw was no fool, just crooked as a dog's hind leg was all. Needham knew Crenshaw took bribes and charged some people more for recording their complaints and writing up affidavits than he charged others. Needham was yet to see the man --or woman -- brave enough to make a public statement against Crenshaw, though. There were those who benefited from underhand deals with him, and they protected him to protect themselves.

Leetch, for instance. Needham didn't know what the payoff to Crenshaw was for not protecting Leetch's apprentices. How many had perished in Leetch's service? Well, the O'Canning boy would not! No sense in wasting a lad like that. Yes, Needham was satisfied that he had done the right thing to go in there and get the boy out. Still, he expected there would be a ruckus before it was over. Leetch had boasted that the girls would be punished, calling for whipping or the stocks for the boy's sister, since she had no goods from which to pay a fine. And the rogue's eyes had gleamed describing the Morgin girl's horse. Leetch and Crenshaw counted on the court awarding the animal to them as "damages" they suffered from the break-in and assaults.

In the back of his mind, "Young" Squire Needham dreaded the fire that "Old" Squire Needham would pour on his head over this "innerference" with other folk's affairs. "Live and let live," Father was always saying, whenever Brant saw someone breaking the law or taking advantage of someone who could not protect themselves. "There's enough strife in the world already without you stirring up more." Brant more often than not would argue that people who were wronged would sooner or later lash out at the people who were doing them wrong, and that would make a lot more trouble and strife. There was no winner in these father-son arguments, but somehow Brant would not give in. Now he was doing it again, even bringing home this lad, another man's apprentice. Yes, Brant Needham the Younger expected grief from his old man.

The young squire was not worried about how his wife would feel about his bringing home a sick boy, more work for her. That was the joy of the man's life, how his wife believed, really believed, in the things he wanted to do, even when they met disfavor from others. She understood his ways and his longings. And he thought he understood her's. He surely tried. How could he not, when she sought out his deepest thoughts, knowing by instinct they were his alone. She never challenged his father's demand that Brant "be like other men." That was not her way. Speaking up to Brant's father would only make life harder in the family. But her admiration of Brant, along with her honest advice, were more a comfort and help to him than a hard mouth to the old man would have been. Brant wondered if his father held her to blame for their not having a son. Brant admitted to himself that it was a sorrow to him. He and his wife did not speak of it, and he did not know if she felt the sorrow or not. He didn't think he would love a son more than he loved their girl, maybe not even as much. But a man in this new country needed a son. More than one would be even better. His father flaunted his own three sons before the world like they were a counter top covered with Spanish milled dollars, all polished and unchipped, fresh from the mint at Segovia. The other two had sons of their own, plenty of Needhams to furnish Carolina, while he, the firstborn and with the old man's name, still had not proved his full manhood in that way.

How had his mind wandered off like this? He had the apprentice boy home now, and a full job of work to see after him, even though he was another man's son, and a dead man's at that.

At the Sheriff's

The compound at Sheriff Night's was spread out like the buildings at the Toliver place. Each building likely had a purpose, but Lizzy couldn't tell right off what they were. A long hitching post was the first thing they came to, and Squire Crenshaw tied up his horse and Copper. Horseshoe made a show of securing his horse to the post. A knotty-looking boy brought up a bucketful of water and poured it into the trough the horses could reach --the biggest hollowed-out tree Lizzy had seen. The boy stared at the two girls, still tied at the wrists. Crenshaw untied their ropes and pushed them toward the house by their shoulders.

The porch ran all across the front of the house, and it had benches, the rough type, some of them sections of tree stumps. Lizzy guessed they were for visitors waiting to see the sheriff. She could see steps down beside the porch leading to a heavy door. Maybe that was the cellar where she and Ruly would be put. The door was low, so there might not be room beyond it to stand up. No doubt the floor would be dirt. At least, she and Ruly would be together. She tried to pay no attention to the questions that rushed to her mind. One thing at a time, girl, just pay attention to what's happening now.

As they walked across the porch to the door on the left side, where people went into the house, Lizzy caught her breath. The house was shaped up so much like Mother's house had been. There were two rooms opening to the porch, a smaller one on the left and a larger one on the right. Mother had used the smaller one, (she called it "the hall") to see her customers when they came for yarn, cloth, or the sewing she did for them. That was where she put her finished goods when they were ready to "go out." The big room, "the parlour," was where they lived and worked and where their company would come.

So it was here. The sheriff used his hall for the public room, and Lizzy guessed the larger room was for his family and their company. His hall had a desk and one chair, with two shelves behind it holding stacks of papers. Higher up, a shelf held two satchels, binding cords, and knives. Lizzy wondered where he bought his paper and how much he paid for it! It felt good to think, even for a second, about something other than the trouble they were in.

Horseshoe had rapped at the open door, but they stayed on the porch till the sheriff came in from the back of the house and called out, "Herschel, what vileness have you arrested now? Gals been in your henhouse? Smokehouse? Or did they come around to catch Horseshoe and show him some fancy tricks with women?"

"Snipes, I've put my day into a serious matter, and I'll expect ye to treat it so. I have affidavies here from Rasco Leetch and his wife charging these wenches with breaking and entering the apprentice quarters of Leetch's shop and with assault and battery of their persons. I have described the knife cuts and bruises Leetch bears from trying to protect his property, his wife, himself, and his apprentice from their trespass and foul intentions. All is writ up proper to put before a grand jury next court. I request ye hold them fast till that time. Ye can see they have no money for bond. They likely stole the horse they rode, and I will volunteer to be its custodian until this be settled."

Sheriff Snipes Night made out like he was sorry and embarrassed in front of Squire Crenshaw. Lizzy wondered why. After his jokey greeting to Crenshaw, he seemed unable to say what he thought Crenshaw wanted him to say. Lizzy guessed that the sheriff was not used to apologizing, which was what she saw him do right now. He spoke low and close to Crenshaw, not looking him in the face. Night was good-looking, not tall but easy in his body and wiry, like he could move fast and never trip up or fall. His dark hair needed washing, and his front teeth were gapped but clean-looking. Lizzy liked his look and wondered if he were as much in cahoots with Crenshaw --and Leetch --as she expected him to be.

By now, she was making sense of his talk. For one thing, it was making Crenshaw really mad. Night was talking about Mr. Marshall! He had come to see the sheriff more than once about Davo, trying to get Night to go with him to Leetch's to see about the boy, after Crenshaw, as the nearest JP, had refused! It seemed Marshall had not given up. Lord, bless him, Lizzy's heart sang out. Saying nothing, she glanced at Ruly. Her friend was looking at the floor, but her wide eyes told Lizzy she understood the good news.

"So the cussed fool took his busy-bodying to young Needham an' got him to interfere in Leetch's right to his apprentice after I turned him down. Snipes, something's got to be done about Marshall. He needs to be charged with something and fined hard, or a crowd of respectable fellows ought to run him off some night. Don't worry, we wouldn't tell you."

"Hershel, you better get it in your head that Daniel Marshall is no fool. True, he's a nuisance, all the time helping people who good men are making good money on. He sets a bad example for society, giving folks notions against their betters. He may be innocent as a dove, but he's shrewd as a serpent. And he knows the law as well as I do."

"Damn you, Snipes! Our lot got you in as sheriff, and you are beholden to protect our interests. You can't stay sheriff long if Marshall gets away with his interfering." Crenshaw cracked his knuckles and let out two deep breaths, then with his eyes narrowed on the sheriff he spat out his words: "I put my whole day into carrying out the law. I ort to at least get the horse."

"We don't yet know it's stolen. Inquiry has to be made. That much is law, and Marshall knows it."

"Law, my arse!" Crenshaw raged afresh. "What exactly do the papers Marshall brought you from Needham say?"

"I told you." Sheriff Night spoke louder now, not caring that the girls heard.

"First, he will apply to the county court to cancel Leetch's mastery on grounds of abuse and neglect." Quickly, over Crenshaw's reaction, Night continued: "seems Needham went to see the boy very early this morning --must have been right after you picked up the wenches -- and he took the boy home with him until the court meets."

Crenshaw looked stunned. "So, he'll tell the court that he did what I should have done when Marshall came to me first."

"As His Majesty's most nigh officer to the site of the alleged malfeasance." The sheriff finished Crenshaw's statement. "Look, Hersch, I don't know why you're working so hard for Rasco Leetch. But there's no point in charging those girls with anything, unless you can prove they stole something from him. Will Leetch claim the horse is his?"

"He better not! I am due that horse for my efforts. No, Leetch won't block me from it. If Squire High and Mighty Needham the Younger has Leetch's boy in custody till the court meets, then I can hold the horse until the court meets and orders a horse inquiry."

"Hersh, I got to stop you there. The sheriff's paddock is a safe place to hold the horse, and nearer the court house than your place."

"I know what you're about, you scoundrel. You want the feeding fee to go to yer own slimy self. Doing business with Sheriff Snipes ain't what I paid for gettin them other JPs to back you. Yer not worth the paper I spent on this here useless affidavy!" Crenshaw spat out the words as he crumpled the paper, threw it at the sheriff, and spun on his heels to leave.

Lizzy heard Horseshoe run along the porch after his father. What would happen next? Would the sheriff let them go, and if he did, how long would it take them to get home without Copper?

The sheriff turned toward his desk and let out a long breath. "All right, you two. Come over here and tell me your names and who you belong to." As he turned, Lizzy snatched Crenshaw's affidavit and stuffed it under her apron. She did not know why, she just did it.

Night had his quill and ink ready and looked up. "Squire Crenshaw's not filing a charge, so you'll be free to scat on to wherever you belong. You first, he nodded to Ruly.

"My name is Rhulia Morgin, and I live with my pa and brothers near the Red Dog ordinary on Middle Creek. And that is my horse." Then she added, "if you please, Sir." She held her shoulders square and looked straight at him.

"Old Spruce Morgin?" Night looked like he thought something was funny. "Didn't know he had a gal this growed-up. And such a fine horse? His trade must be right good these days."

"We manage. The horse is mine, not Pa's."

"We'll sort that out. Now you," looking at Lizzy.

Lizzy had it all thought out. "I am Elizabeth O'Canning. The apprentice is my brother. I heered he was truly sick, and my friend and I sneaked into Mr. Leetch's shop last night with some broth and medicinals. He was like he was sleeping and couldn't wake up, very poorly. We were treating him when Mrs. Leetch found us and called the squire."

Before she could say more, Night frowned sideways toward her. "The boy is your brother, so you're an orphan, too. I recollect you now. Tomm Toliver wanted you for to lighten the work load of his fancy wife." He was silent, studying Lizzy. It was her turn to look straight ahead and try not to tremble. But she felt herself shake and it made her mad: why couldn't she be like Ruly?

"Not trying to run away now, are you?" the two of you, with a stolen horse, eh? Expected to take the boy with you?

Leetch and Crenshaw both too dumb to figure it out? How now!! What an in-ter-resting kettle of fish I have caught!"

The Ginger-Haired Man

"Sir, please Sir, we want only to return to the Red Dog," Ruly spoke calmly. Mr. Toliver knows his apprentice is with me. It was he who axed me to provide my horse and go with her, and I can prove the horse is mine."

While Ruly spoke, a man looked in from the porch, saw the sheriff was busy, and sat down on one of the benches. "Stay here. I'll deal with you directly." Night strode past the girls toward the newcomer. "Schoolteacher! You're back to stay a while I hope, long enough to wrassle some learning into our domestic savages!" Lizzy glanced toward the porch as the visitor arose, and they shook hands -- like proper gentlemen, she thought. Not the way the sheriff had been with Squire Crenshaw.

"I just came to nail up one of my school announcements on your porch, if I may. I hope to get up a five-week school before I move on back to Jersey. I'm trying to put one at all the places folks accumulate."

Lizzy was startled. She had heard the voice before, and the politeness. Moving to get a better look, she recognized the ginger-haired man she had seen in the Red Dog several times when she first was there.

"Whereabouts you expect to hold school, Powell?"

Lizzy could see now that the ginger-haired teacher was much younger than the sheriff. Maybe about Ruly's age; the thought surprised her as he answered,

"Big Jeff will rent me an airy room in one of his buildings. Folks can pay me with things he can sell, and he and I will settle. They'll have to pay me first, though, and I'll need enough boys and girls to make it pay."

"People know you from your first teaching here, so you'll likely get enough. If the weather holds, you'll be hitting lay-by time just right. Folks may keep their girls home to help dry beans and fruit, but there'll be little field work 'til harvest." He squinted at the schoolteacher and ventured, "I 'spect you'll get 15 or 20 younguns. I'll make men with chil'ren get the meaning of your sign here."

"Obliged to you, Sheriff," and the schoolteacher shook hands to leave.

Lizzy couldn't stand it. This man could tell the sheriff she belonged with the Tolivers – if he could remember her.

"Please Sir," she stepped onto the porch, Ruly right behind her.

"Sir, do you recollect me from the Red Dog public house? I'm the apprentice there. My friend and I need a body to say they know us to satisfy the law." She threw in the "law" part for Night's benefit.

The tall man peered down and smiled. "You're Miss O'Canning! I recall your name because it's like that scoundrel's in Hillsborough – who's no kin of yours," he laughed. Then, to the sheriff, "I do know this girl. She works at the Red Dog public house, down by the Middle Creek crossroads. Her master speaks highly of her."

"And me, Sir," put in Ruly. Don't know me, but ye likely know of my pa, Bruce Morgin. Well, he's generally known as "Spruce" Morgin. Or maybe my oldest brother, Jackson."

The ginger head was nodding. "Yes, I've enjoyed your family's spruce beer, though I don't know them directly." To the sheriff he said, "If it helps these young women, I am glad to verify who they are."

"Know anything about the horse yonder?"

"Don't know the horse."

The sheriff looked at Ruly. "I'm writing the description of the horse, Gal, and if one like it is reported missing, I know where you are. Get along, you two." Lizzy thought he figured the horse belonged to Ruly but was trying to show he was in charge.

Ruly was quick to take the schoolteacher's attention. Lizzy thought her friend was speaking in a syrupy voice when she smiled and said, "Sir, we can take one of yer papers and nail it up at the Red Dog for ye, if ye like."

"That's good, good. I'm heading across to Hinton's Quarter now and up to the Richland settlement and Crabtree. You'll save me a trip down your way." Lizzy thought he was smiling at her – Lizzy – when he added, "Not that stopping in the Red Dog would be unpleasant." He handed two of his papers to Lizzy. "I'm obliged to you, Miss. Give my greeting to Tomm and his wife."

Was it Lizzy's imagination, or had the man remembered her name but not Goody's? She thought on this as they walked towards Copper. Ruly untied him quickly and started leading him back to the road. Lizzy was glad to walk for a while, too, but as soon as they got out of sight of Night's place, she realized why Ruly didn't want them to ride yet. Lizzy had put the paper in her apron pocket, but Ruly demanded:

"He'll have his name on it. I want to know his name! Read it to me." Lizzy read,

Mr. Powell Rednappe, schoolmaster from New Jersey, has returned to friends in Johnston County for a school on weekdays from July 10 through August 10 at Mr. Osborne's. Males and females. Minimum 12 scholars, paid by July 12: 10s in Va. currency or value in merchantable country goods. Reading, writing, cyphering, English grammar, hymns.

"Powell Rednappe," Ruly repeated and laughed. "Well, it fits, with that hair."

"What?"

"Rednappe, silly!" His last name's Rednappe. What a family he must come from." Realizing Lizzy still did not get the joke, Ruly went on, a little embarrassed for her friend. "I declare, Lizzy, with your learnin' you don't know that red-nappe is old-timey talk for a red-head. I don't care about his hair. He's a god-awful good-looking piece of manflesh. And he seems like he'd be good to a woman. He's likely not married yet. Them schoolteachers that moves about like he does, teaching here and there through the country like preachers do, they generally stay single. At least till they settle where they's lots of folk, or they save up to buy land or something. I feature Powell Rednappe is one smart man and apt to make his mark on this world."

Ruly's interest surprised Lizzy. Her feeling was more than surprise, but she didn't know what it was. It was like a drag or a dread. Was Ruly interested in men and marriage already? Of course, Ruly was older than she. Lizzy didn't know how much older, and she never had asked Ruly, not wanting to embarrass her. Ruly might not know, with her mother being dead and her pa being, well, vague. What if Ruly got married and they couldn't visit anymore? Ruly was the best thing in her life, except for Davo, and Ruly had ventured with her to help Davo. She was puzzled what to say. Ruly was quiet, too.

"He does seem goodly." Not liking how that sounded, Lizzy tested the waters. "I didn't know you were interested in getting married already." She held her breath.

"Already!? I would have tore out of that hole two-three years ago if I had a chance. Pa can be so mean to me, and the boys expect me to do whatever they say. Even little Max wants me to wait on him. And Lizzy, you know I ain't lazy. It's not the work. They're just so, so, bully. And sometimes I really am scared o' Pa." Then almost under her breath, "now that I'm grown up. I do need to get out of there." She looked hard and Lizzy. Then sighed, "A kind man would be a sweet thing. I could start out fresh with him. Yeah, I'm up for marrying." She glanced to see Lizzy's reaction, but there was none.

Goody's Surprise

The ride home was restful. For the first time, Lizzy noticed trees with full-sized leaves. The last blooms lingered on the shrubs of horse sugar, and ripe mayapples showed in their patches. She realized she had missed seeing them at their best from worry and work. They left the road twice, to follow a wet place to a stream for Copper to drink. There was a world of putty root, their faded leaves showing it was a good time to take up the "Adam and Eve" from the roots, early enough for more of them to grow. Goody could use these! While the horse drank, she dug under several plants with a stick and gathered enough to please the old fire-eater. With days lengthening now, maybe they could get to the Red Dog while it was still light. Lizzy was so relieved to be out of trouble that she enjoyed the greening day and did not dread Goody's tongue.

Wa'ro saw them first. He took Copper to feed and rub him down, and the girls went straight to the kitchen. Goody was there all right, but she did not rile up at all. Fact is, Goody looked peaked and just said "Glad yer home. Lots of pots to scrub tonight." She had saved them up for Lizzy; nearly all Goody's cooking things were dirty. "Afore ye do, go show yersels to Tomm, the both o' ye."

"I'll be right back to do the pots." Somehow Lizzy felt sorry for Goody, maybe because she did not scold them.

When they saw Tomm behind the counter, he did not look like himself. He was his usual cheerful and talking self, but something about the way he carried himself had changed. He stood higher, seemed more energetic, high in his spirit. He looked younger. Lizzy never wondered how old he and Goody were, but this was younger than she thought. He looked twice when they entered, probably expecting his wife.

"Gulls! Ye be back, praise God! Yer brother? How be he?"

Lizzy couldn't tell it all right there and just said they found him near dead and treated him, but his master (she did not say Leetch's name, lest she be overheard) caught them, charged them with crimes and sent them to the sheriff but he let them go free.

"Let ye go, did he? Ye gulls must 'a done some mighty talking?" His look went to Ruly, thinking it was her wit that got them off.

"We had help, Tomm. The schoolteacher Mr. Rednappe happened by and recognized Lizzy. Otherwise, Night would 'a put us in his cellar and impounded Copper as stolen." Ruly knew that big word from listening at court, Lizzy reckoned.

"So young Rednappe is back in this parts. Last winter he said he was going to Orange and Rowan to try for schools at the new settlements and then work his way back through here before heading to Virginny. His rounds get wider with all this settlement going on."

Lizzy brought out the papers about the school, handed one to Ruly to take to Lincoln's pottery place, and asked if she could put one in the Red Dog. Tomm nodded.

Back at the kitchen, Ruly helped with the scrubbing and said she would spend the night. They had been working a while when Goody spoke from the chimney corner. "Eat up afore ye finish, and ye can warsh all o' the plates. I should o' told you to eat already." She added weakly, "I'm a mite diverted, I am."

Lizzy ventured to ask how Goody was feeling, sure that something was wrong.

Excited suddenly, Goody whispered, "If ye'll bind yersels by holy oath on your mother's soul – both o' ye -- that ye'll not tell—I'll tell ye. I dassn't have nobody to know this thing afore time. . . . Well?"

"I never took an oath, Goody, but I can promise faithfully."

'S not good enough. If ye keep yer oath, there be no danger at all in it."

"I'll swear. Lizzy, you jest to what I do." Ruly was in a hurry to know.

"All'ight. On yer knees, cross fingers, cross hands over yer heart, look up t'ward the east, it's yonder winder," and she pointed.

They did, and she let forth a stream of words, slowly so they could repeat, including "codsnails", "my own mother's soul", "Cheezus-Charusalem", and "eternal damnation." Lizzy did not like it, and she did not speak out all the words. Ruly seemed to know the ritual and spoke loud so Lizzy could hide her own words. Lizzy looked scared enough to satisfy Goody.

"All'ight. Here 'tis. Gull, you will be doing more work, as I shall lighten my load a bit." Lizzy could not imagine what "load" of work Goody had been doing all these months. "Here be it, now. I be with child. You heered me right. Suspicioned it a while, and now I know." Desperately curious, Lizzy blurted, "HOW do you know?" She had no idea. Ruly kept quiet.

Right off, Lizzy wished she could call back her girlish question. Tomm had told her about four babies dying, but Goody did not know she knew. Goody did not seem to be bothered, though, and simply said, "Yer menses quit for one t'ing, and yer bosoms feel bruised-like and pain ye. Some gets sick ever morning, throwin' up bad, but t'at quits after a while. This was news to Lizzy, and her face must have showed sorrow, for Goody allowed as how "'twould all be worth it, and more, if a baby be strong enough to live to grow up in 'is world."

Lizzy didn't know what to say, but Ruly chimed out, "I'm real proud for ye, Miz Goody, and for Mr. Tomm. Lizzy's here to help ye, and yer a fulsome hearty woman, with good looks and all. No wonder yer man's good seed has sprouted. Ye'll be a fine family for sure."

"It'll be grand to have a little 'un here, Goody. Tomm and 'Ro and I will be mighty pleased."

"'Ro don't know, mind you. He'd take the news to the McBee place, then ever'body 'tween the 'Lantic and the Yadkin 'ud know."

"Speaking of the widow, Miz Goody, do ye think it would be a comfort to have her and her woman call on ye about how the baby's comin' along, not right now I mean, but when ye'r ready to tell folks. I hear her woman knows a lot and sometimes births babies."

Goody lifted her head and thought. "I might want to get that Minerva here afore I tell it. She knows sprit t'ings, I'm told. I could tell it if she t'inks the baby will prosper. Thank you, Ruly. You be a smarter gull that I knew." Ruly did not understand the compliment, but Lizzy did. Goody would feel confident if Minerva judged her baby to be sound.

"'Ro won't have to know what you're calling her for if he goes to get her." Lizzy thought she was being helpful.

"That Cicero has plenty of work to do without traipsing to the widow's. I'll see a woman in the Red Dog who'll take a message to the widow for me. Time enough."

Goody's news was all the girls talked about before they fell asleep on Lizzy's straw. "Why are ye so surprised, Lizz-O? They be man and woman."

"But they're so old. I never thought this would happen." Lizzy thought maybe this was what Tomm had meant when he told Lizzy about the four babies and that Goody had "given up."

"Folks can go on having babies a long time. I heered my Pa say my mother was not yet forty when she died having Max, and Goody's not that old."

"But she looks older. The strange colors on her skin, the spots, even the way she walks."

"Goody got too much sun on her in early years, that's for sure. And some white people just be extra pale, specially when they got red hair, and it makes spots and wrinkles faster'n others. Didn't you know that?" Well, no, Lizzy didn't know that. "And about the walkin', well she don't walk bent over when she's around other people. You watch her." Ruly was indeed a watcher. Also, Lizzy had never seen Goody's hair uncovered, beyond the sprigs around her face. Those mushroom eyes, though. Lizzy had never got past thinking they were hair-raising. "And the reds and pinks on her skin," Ruly went on, "they just be something she saw pretty up another woman. She likely don't notice it makes her look older. And if Tomm Toliver likes it, well, who else matters?"

They got quiet, listening to the whip-poor-wills, whose calls had slowed since their frenzied start-up weeks earlier.

"Well, how old do you think Tomm is?" Lizzy didn't add what she was thinking: *since you know every little thing.*

"Oh, I reckon him to be not yet thirty-five." Most bowlegged folks get that way when they're chil'ren. They just look like they been ridin' cows fer years."

For the next three or four months, Lizzy felt a new ease and calm. The court had given Davo's apprenticeship to Squire Needham! He was teaching the boy to read, write, and cypher, and a loom maker close by was training him to make looms, spinning wheels, and light joinery. The only things that clouded

Lizzy's mind were Goody's sickliness and some dissatisfaction about Wa'ro that nagged her.

The two worries came together after the Widow McBee and Minerva started calling on Goody. Minerva seemed almost as interested in Lizzy as in Goody's troubles. Lizzy was glad for the interest and returned it, but it puzzled her. The first time Minerva came, Lizzy thanked her for the medicinals she had sent for Davo, and she added that Davo was living with young Squire Needham now. The woman did not smile but glanced at the girl, allowing as how it was always good when a body got out of a bad situation. The glance seemed to mean something, but what? Lizzy had a dull feeling that something more dangerous and lonely than rescuing Davo lay ahead.

Passes?

Lizzy loved seeing the Widow McBee up close. She was kind to Goody and cheerful all around, but she wasted no time, worked fast, and did not gossip. Lizzy liked that. First time they came, Minerva took the lead, questioning Goody, feeling about on her body, nodding every once in a while, and finally announcing to Mrs. McBee, "Hummph, Umm, umm, um." The widow seemed to know what Minerva meant and asked, "Can we get what we need?" "Yes'sum" was Minerva's only reply, and she headed for the door and went to Wa'ro, like she had something to say to him. After the first few visits, the widow left Minerva at home, saying her helper had "cased up" Goody's troubles and made the right medicinals. Mrs. McBee brought fresh supplies and helped Goody use them. Lizzy had wondered if she would be needed for this her own self, but she was not. It was all between the widow and Goody, now that Minerva had worked it out. They got into a habit, Mrs. McBee coming early and staying with Goody just long enough to take care of her and to drink a little dandelion tea Lizzy had ready for them. The girl brought butter or honey and whatever bits of bread were at hand, hoping to get Mrs. McBee to stay longer that way, and she did, a little. Lizzy did not drink tea with them, but Mrs.

McBee always thanked her. More and more, she told Lizzy what to watch for about Goody, but she did not let Goody hear her. "Send Cicero if she swells up, or swoons, or has trouble walking or keeping food down." Later she told Lizzy, "You're a sensible girl. I won't come so often now. When Goody's time gets close, I'll send Minerva, or if Goody has trouble before then. Lizzy felt the weight of that, but it was pleasing that Mrs. McBee confidenced her. Would Lizzy ever be as smart and in control of herself? She even imagined sometime that after the apprenticeship she might find spinning work with the widow or get a start with someone she sent her to. She felt proud of having her confidence.

Ruly came around more often, too. Not to see Lizzy, though, but bringing things to Goody, sometimes offering to help Lizzy with the washing. Lizzy did have more work now, and Ruly's time with Goody relieved her. Goody did not go to the Red Dog anymore. She ventured to the kitchen and sat and peeled and cut up things for Lizzy. She still did not want to talk about having a baby. Lizzy and Tomm understood why. Lizzy wondered if Ruly knew but did not ask. Wa'ro was extra helpful, too, with things he could do. He even carried some heavy platters of food to the Red Dog, maybe to make sure they would not be broken by a clumsy girl. Wa'ro spoke little, seemed to have is mind far-off. What was it, Lizzy wondered. Then one day he told her.

"Miss Lizzy, I have a matter to speak. It is a dangerous thing, and you could get me killed or sold away from here if you told anybody." Lizzy was shocked at how much better he talked, realizing she had not hear him talk for a while. He must have learned it from his girlfriend, for her mother's talking was careful and clear. Then she thought about his words: killed or sold off if she told?

"No, Wa'ro, you know you can trust me. What is it??" The matter he told her was nothing less than he and Ahmee wanted to run off together and live free, and they had a notion of where they could go: to one of the swamps on the other side the Tarr River, toward the sun's rising.

"How can you do such a thing?"

"That's where we need you, Miss Lizzy."

"How do you aim to go about it? No, first, how do you know about the swamps and how to get to them? Folks hide out sometimes in the swamps near here, but they either come out or get found! Where is such a swamp you would not be found, and stay there forever?" It seemed an impossible dream.

"Well," he began, "We know about it 'cause some of Ahmee's connection told us, they even went there to see and came back and can tell us how to get there." Who would do that, Lizzy wondered – have enough freedom to go, and then be willing to come back? Sometime later she would think, "Gaspar!" Now she was too shocked to think.

"It's not enough to run off and meet one another. You got to get there without being seen. You will be missed. Tomm and the widow will call for a hunt, you know that. They won't just let you go. You're too valuable, young healthy people, no. You'd get caught, 'Ro, and you'd be separated and sold away for sure, likely after a hard whipping." Lizzy started to cry. It was a good thing they were out of sight and sound of the house. They were hauling water to wash. 'Ro usually filled the pots himself, but Lizzy helped so they could have their heads together and talk while walking. They set the bucket-log down between them by the steam.

"Miss Lizzy, you got to understand. I love her. I got to be with her." The veins in Wa'ro's neck stood out, and its muscles looked tight enough to lift a whole wash pot full of water. His face looked like it would explode. Lizzy could feel his heat and power, being that close. "Mr. Tomm and the widow would let us marry and visit each other," he went on, "but we don't want to be living like that. 'Sides, our children would belong to the widow. How long she going to live? Ahmee and children would be sold, likely not to the same place. No. I won't have it. I won't. And she's the same mind as me."

"So, you both run off, but what's next? How you going to hide yourselves all that way, even when you think you know the way? And are there other people in this swamp you're thinking about? Will they let you in?"

"Yes, there are. People got there same way we want to. They ran and hid, hid and ran, till they got to where folks like them let them stay. They raise food, fish and hunt, and help one another. They even got preachers and healers. And some white women that don't do them any harm come and go and handle trade with the outside." Lizzy had no notion that this kind of thing could be. More slowly, he said, "What we need, Miss Lizzy, is some passes."

"Passes?"

"Papers, with writing to say we have our owners' say-so to travel. It would need our names, and Miz McBee and Mr. Tomm's names, too. So anybody stop us, we can show who we are and say we are on business for our owners." They were back at the wash pot now, and Lizzy was thinking on all he had said while they emptied up the bucket-log. Finally she whispered what came to her, "Are you thinking I can get you two passes?"

"You got good paper. That's a start." He headed back to the stream with the bucket, leaving her to think further.

Paper and ink for forging passes: these Lizzy had. Plus, she could write. She could work out what to say in the papers, but whose name could she put at the bottom? What name to make folks believe the passes? She tried to remember: had any justice or constable signed a chit or a ledger in the Red Dog that she could copy? She thought not. She, Goody, or Tomm did the writing. That thinking brought to mind the affidavit Crenshaw had thrown down at the sheriffs – and Lizzy had picked up! Zounds, was it still caught in her clothes all this time? She dared not tell Wa'ro yet that a possible plan was forming, but her mind raced ahead. The affidavit was in Crenshaw's hand, with his signature. She had paper to practice on until she got to writing like him, and then she could write out passes and put his name on them. The thought made her nearly sick with fear. This was not a prank. She would have to think long on this, and when Wa'ro returned with more water, she promised she would put her mind to what he needed.

In the Corner of Her Eye

That night, Lizzy tossed in the straw, tired but unable to sleep from thinking about what she was thinking about doing. She had found the crushed affidavit, and as she had studied it, it had felt like lightening in her hands. Would she really forge a pass that would deprive Tomm of a worker he had paid for and treated well, and do the same injustice to the Widow McBee? Both were good people. They were kind to her and others, and fair. Lizzy looked up to them. The thought of betraying them shocked and scared her. Why was she even thinking of forging passes? It would be dishonest. The thought made her feel dirty! It was against the law, and the law was harsh when it suited the JPs to enforce it. She had seen that in the one court she saw. Chasing that thought, she wondered how Elke Tikell's baby was doing at the McBee place and if Elke ever got to see him. It was all up to what the widow would allow, wasn't it? That brought Lizzy back to the widow's seeming kindness. But why couldn't other women be as free as the widow, women who did not have her money or the good name of a dead hero-husband? Something was stacked against all poor people, nearly all Negro people, and most women. Who made it that way? Had God done it at the beginning of time? She could not think Jesus could be any part of it. Was it the king? Was it like this with other people? She wondered about the Occaneechi, Cherokees, and Wa'ro's people back where he came from. All these thoughts made her tumble more, till her bones felt the hard floor.

She sat up and hugged her knees. What would Mother do? What would Mr. Marshall do? She dare not confide in Mr. Marshall. That would put him in the same hard spot she was in. Besides, she had promised Wa'ro not to tell, and that was that. Mother? She would give it a good thinking-through, Lizzy knew that, and that is what Lizzy was doing. Mother would pray, she remembered that. The thought calmed her. Certainly, her mother would not wear out her bones all over the floor, fretting. There was a difference between worrying and thinking.

She thought she remembered Mother say that. Or had that just come to Lizzy from inside her own self? Was that praying? Lizzy loved the true dark, like now. The cloudy night sky sent only a breeze through the shutter, without a crack of light. She sat there, thinking of herself as a pinpoint of a person in the endless, comforting, darkness that held her close to where she needed to be. Was this praying? The fleeting thought pleased her but did not linger.

Without meaning to, she rose and walked to the window, remembering the way without trying, and opened the shutter a little more. She smelled, then tasted, the moist night. If I don't write the passes, she thought, Wa'ro and Ahmee will run anyway. Passes would make their safety more likely. Without focusing her eyes, she thought she saw figures on the ground beneath the oaks. A small circle of children, hands linked and playing a game. She knew it was the breeze moving last year's leaves, but while the image stayed with her, the corner of an eye saw a cabin, a stream, and two adults. That's how it could be, she thought. Amen.

Next day, she started learning to write like Squire Hershel Crenshaw.

Ahmee's Raft

Wa'ro told Ahmee about the passes next time he was at the widow's. Tomm sent him on Snap, to get him shod by the farrier at the McBee place, a tall Ibo man who had worked with iron all his life, like Wa'ro's father. Nestor had been in Carolina since he was younger than Wa'ro, but he had lived at Campbelton with a nephew of Colonel McBee a few years, long enough to not sicken when the seasons changed and to learn how the people there talked. Sometimes Nestor traveled with Gaspar when the widow sent Gaspar to buy or sell horses. The farrier told Wa'ro about places he had been and the habits of people he saw. Wa'ro liked the man and tried to remember everything he said.

When Wa'ro told Ahmee that Lizzy was learning to forge a JP's hand so she could make passes for them, Ahmee seemed relieved but not surprised. It was like she expected Lizzy to do it eventually but not right away. Wa'ro did not understand, but he could see the girl's excitement that the time would be soon. Ahmee had made several escape plans, and her favorite was the one they chose. It was then Wa'ro realized that Ahmee's parents wanted them to escape together, for she had talked about it with them! Gaspar and Minerva had to cover themselves so the widow would never suspect they knew. Wa'ro gasped: "We're really going to get away and be together."

The McBee place was south of Big Jeff Osborne's place and reached Green's Path. It included where the path crossed the Tarr River. The headquarters where the widow and her people lived was about a mile west of the river, and there were thick trees along a stretch of the bank. That is where Ahmee intended to build a raft. She knew the place well enough to slip out before dawn and work a while in the mornings before she was expected at the house, and daylight still came early. Gaspar already had taken lumber and leather to the spot, and she knew how to lash rafts. She had made rafts for the widow. It would be foolish to take one of the widow's rafts, for that would tell everyone that they were floating down the Tarr. When Wa'ro had the passes and she had the raft ready, they would strike out.

They hoped to raft down the river almost to Tarr Burrow, a settlement where several paths came together. They would hide the raft and walk the paths like they were confident and get across the river in the little settlement. Gaspar told Ahmee how to take another road out of the village as quickly as possible. Their goal was a large high swamp between Tarr Burrow and Conneta Creek. Gaspar had been there once while he was out travelling for the widow, and he had talked with people who had tried to get there but had been caught, brought back, and punished.

Wa'ro thought on how Ahmee's parents were helping her do something that would make it impossible to see her again and how that must feel. Miz Minerva had to be in on it, he knew, but you would never know by the way she acted. He hoped Ahmee had learned much of her mother's ways with medicinals and spirit doings. They would need special knowledge. Also, he wondered if Ahmee was ready for this kind of risk, or for that matter, if he were. Yes, he believed he was, knowing how much he wanted freedom and Ahmee. She was younger, and she had never been away from her people, as he was. Would she hold up for the escape and for living in a swamp, away from all she knew?

For all the next month and more, Ahmee worked on a raft every morning she saw a chance. Sometimes Mrs. McBee had early work for her, but Ahmee usually knew the night before. She was surprised how quickly the raft was ready, and then she was impatient to know about the passes. She strapped the raft well with strong leather and sealed it tight with wax from candle ends. Two poles she shaped stood ready to reach the river bottom as needed to move the raft along. She covered her finished work with live vines that would remain green until she took it off.

During this time, Minerva went to care for Goody once, but she did not so much as look at Wa'ro. He admired her self-control. She brought a basket of dried raspberry leaves from the widow's vines to make tea that helped women bring on their babies. The raspberries did not grow wild, and Minerva believed raspberry tea did more good than tea from the green nettles that Lizzy gathered for her.

Minerva was surprised that Goody already knew how to soak bones in cider vinegar to make a brew that would strengthen the baby's bones. Goody took a tablespoon in a glass of water every day. She told Minerva she had wanted a baby for a long time and had figured out how to get one. Keeping her face serious, Minerva laughed inside, but she knew what Goody meant: she had been eating special berries and roots that she thought would help her get with child. Minerva offered no advice, as none was asked, and besides, it had worked: Goody was with child. Minerva did wonder, though, if Goody was still eating the roots and berries. Some of them were harmful after a baby had started forming. Minerva noticed that Goody was partial to certain foods, too. The main one was pokeweed. Lizzy cooked the leaves in two waters, threw out the waters and then cooked the greens down a third time to make a soft, tasty "sallit." Goody ate it by heaps. Minerva knew good uses for the berries and root of the poke plant, but she warned Goody that women with babies coming needed to stay away from pokeberries. That was as far as Minerva would go in telling Goody what to do, and Goody did not take it well.

She looked at Minerva like she wanted her to mind her own business but remembered that Minerva was there to help her, sent by Mrs. McBee out of kindness, and Goody felt small about that. Nobody knew it, but pokeberries were where Goody got the pink color for her cheeks, lips, and shoulders. She would look a pale sight if she did not use the berry juice. She even dried them for winter and soaked them in water, one at a time, to have the coloring. Minerva need not know about that. Goody was six years older than Tomm, but nobody knew it, not even Tomm, and she was keeping it that way. Having this baby would keep up her idea of being young forever. The milk would make her breasts even bigger, and she would be proud of that. She had eaten the berries of monk's pepper for a year to help her get a baby, and she still took them, to be on the sure side. Nobody knew that, either. She still ate the dried cohosh she had saved up, too. She had made up her mind to have a baby, and have it she would.

Goody stayed in bed most of the time. It seemed to Lizzy that this was more of Goody's laziness, taking advantage of her condition. So did Ruly, who came more often but spent most of her time doing things for Goody. Tomm petted his wife more and brought her what she wanted. He was so pleased about the baby that he took her weakness as normal. Minerva was the only person to suspect something was wrong. Lizzy's days and evenings were spent washing, cleaning, cooking, and serving in the Red Dog with Tomm. She expected there would be more work once the baby was born. She admitted to herself that Wa'ro would no longer be there if their plan worked, and that would put more work on her. She tried not to think about that.

None of these worries got her down, for two reasons. First, Davo was safe. Squire Needham brought him to see Lizzy a few weeks after he got him from Leetch's. He looked so much better! No longer skinny, and his hair was starting to grow again. He told her Mrs. Needham was a grand woman, like Mother. She had explained that the thing growing on his head was not really a worm, though people called it that. Keeping it clean and in clean air had made it go away, and the salve Lizzy had brought from Minerva helped the pain and itching, so he did not scratch anymore. Davo was almost himself again, Lizzy thought. There was something new about him, though – something wary and cunning, like he could be mean. She wondered if it would go away after he got used to being safe. Still, Davo's improvement and his safety with Squire Needham was the big thing that made Lizzy happy.

The other thing was that she believed she could help Wa'ro and Ahmee be free and safe. Late at night, she pulled a small table to the fire and practiced copying Squire Crenshaw's writing. She filled both sides of a paper and then burned it so no one would see it. Every night it looked a little more like his writing, and this made her proud and hopeful. She went to sleep in that mind every night.

One morning, she woke extra early. She felt rested but excited. She would make the passes right now, without thinking a lot. Already she had written them in her mind, over and over. She built up the fire a bit, gathered her ink and paper, and lit a candle stub. Calmly, she wrote out two passes and folded each one. She felt like she was imagining it, but there they were! She folded each a second time and dripped candle wax on the loose edges, to make it impossible to read without opening the wax seal. While the wax was hot, she lay the quill across each seal twice, making a cross. After the wax hardened, she wrapped each pass in a small piece of linen and fastened it with a wood splinter. She would keep them in her pocket until she slipped them to Wa'ro that very day.

"I made a separate pass for each of you, giving your owner's name and saying you are on their business and can travel in Johnston, Edgecombe, Pitt, and Halifax counties." She spoke fast as he tucked them inside his jacket. "The one with the longer splinter is Ahmee's." Lizzy wanted to say so much more, but no words came, and her voice broke.

"Our first girl will be Elizabeth." Wa'ro's serious gaze moved from the grass up to Lizzy's face. Two days later, Minerva showed up at the Tolivers' place. Lizzy had no idea how Wa'ro had got in touch with Ahmee.

The purpose of Minerva's visit, she said, was to make a cold posset for Goody, something she had mentioned earlier. She had told Tomm to have musk ready, and so he had killed two male muskrats and removed the secretions from their glands. Already Goody had on hand the rose water, white wine, and rosemary Minerva required. She had promised to come make the posset when the unripe grapes at the McBee place reached a certain point. She needed two lemons as well. The McBee's contacts with Campbelton and Cross Creek brought lemons occasionally, and the widow sold her extra ones to Tomm to use at the Red Dog. Minerva declared that a cold posset in the heat of the summer was the thing a lady with child needed most, and she made much of the timing for having both the lemons and the juice of green grapes, which she called "verges." Lizzy admired the cleverness of Ahmee's mother now more than ever. Using milk fresh from the cow, Minerva mixed her ingredients, steeped them like making tea, and then let them cool. She told Goody to drink a dish several times a day and at night until she used it all. Then Minerva left, as quietly has she had arrived, and no doubt, Lizzy thought, with Ahmee's pass in her clothing.

The following morning, Wa'ro and his few clothes were gone. The trip was longer without a horse, and he had left at first dark. He found Ahmee waiting at the raft, enveloped in the moonless night. A closed basket of doves slept noiselessly beside her.

Foxing the Widow

No one noticed that Ahmee was gone for about an hour after she normally would be seen. Minerva, usually the first to see her daughter, had left before day to begin pulling up the flax plants. With Mrs. McBee's concurrence, she started at the most distant planting in order to minimize her time in the hot sun, either in the field or in the donkey cart that carried her and the flax stooks. She took molasses biscuits and did not return until almost night, after spreading the flax near a stream about half a mile from the quarters. She hoped that when the widow realized Ahmee had gone off, she would think the girl had left with her mother and then fled westward beyond the Neuse River. Ahmee's job that day was to pluck feathers from geese, a task that required her to be outdoors. Minerva had left biscuits wrapped on the table, beside the molasses jug, as though waiting to be Ahmee's breakfast. That is what Widow McBee saw after she noticed the undisturbed geese and started looking for Ahmee.

Gaspar had planned for his own absence on the day of his daughter's escape. Like Minerva, he also hoped to misdirect Mrs. McBee. In her shock of seeing that Ahmee's clothes were missing and her breakfast untouched, the widow remembered Gaspar's request of the previous evening. Soon after Minerva returned from the Toliver's the day before, Gaspar had come to the widow and offered to take the supply wagon to Osborne's the next day so that the boy who usually made that trip could work with the blacksmith. The trader who brought iron bars had been late getting to the McBee place, because late spring freshets had damaged the iron works where he got the iron. Now Mrs. McBee's smith was behind in his work. As the widow had no urgent task for Gaspar or the boy, she had approved. Now with Ahmee gone, the owner suspected that Gaspar had left extra early, hiding Ahmee, perhaps in an empty cask.

The widow asked herself what direction Ahmee would take from anywhere around Osborne's? It was believed that runaways fled towards the mountains to the north and west, but those were hazardous places. If she headed for the mountains, she would do well to stay off the paths if she could, for the country was getting peopled up in Granville and Orange. It was easier to hide by following the streams as they narrowed, but snakes and other vermin infested those waters this time of year. Ahmee would not likely be alone, Mrs. McBee thought. There were girls and boys Ahmee's age who came here with the widow's relatives to the east. If they had planned to meet and run together, that would be more reason to flee westward. This was exactly what Gaspar wanted the widow to think.

The idea that Ahmee had run away shocked and hurt her owner. Ahmee was a privileged Negro in a privileged family! It unsettled Mrs. McBee even more that Gaspar would have connived with her!! The widow ordered herself to keep her head. Where was Minerva today? Oh, yes, the flax; innocent enough, until she thought about the flax fields' being out of sight. The fields lay near two paths, either of which would lead straight to that Cicero who belonged to the Tolivers! If Ahmee hid during the day, she could meet Cicero somewhere down there and take off toward the Black River and any number of swamps. The widow had heard of Negroes living in the swamps, and the country to the south was full of them. Which way? To the north and west, likely with Gaspar's help, or to the south, with Minerva's?

Margaret McBee would not be foxed! She would send a message to all the JPs around, and she would send reward notices to the *North Carolina Gazette* and the *Virginia Gazette* and even to the paper in Charles Town. That took time, but all three papers were passed about through the backcountry. Ahmee was too good to lose. The widow never intended to sell her, or any of her close Negroes, and the girl had learned bee-keeping, dairying, linen-making, and medicinals from Minerva and cleverness from both parents; too clever, the widow thought. She wrote her message to JPs and decided on Nestor to circulate it. She would wait until Gaspar and Minerva returned, in case she had misjudged them.

A thought crushed her spirit even further: what if the parents, too, had fled? Unthinkable. But was it really less likely that Ahmee's parents would have helped her escape to where they would not see her again? More reason to suppose the family had gone off together. She knew Gaspar understood the country well and was astonished that she had poisoned her own stream by trusting him so much! How could he and Minerva do this, and why? She knew she treated them better than most folks with Negroes treated them: a good house, privileges, plenty of food, and work they like. Why, why? For the first time in her life, the Widow McBee felt alone and helpless. Not even the colonel's death had hit her this hard. She felt violated and undone. She headed for the enclosure where Ahmee's brother was supposed to be training horses. He was there!

At the Red Dog, Lizzy milked as usual the next morning but said nothing about 'Ro not being there. They would miss him soon enough. As soon as she strained the milk and took care of it, she took Goody's posset to her. The girl wondered if the "cold posset," as Minerva had called it, was really helpful. She thought it might be something Minerva used as an excuse to come and get Ahmee's pass. Mayhap it was both. Lizzy determined to think little about it and be surprised when they learned that 'Ro was gone.

It did not take long. Tomm rushed in from the stable, asking for the boy and saying his clothes were gone. His pale face said he knew he had run away, even before he spoke.

Goody sat up straight in the bed. The horses? Are the horses safe? The whiskey? Before Tomm could say nothing was missing, Goody whipped out of bed, ran out the door, let loose a stream of sounds Lizzy had never heard. She must be cursing in Irish Gaelic, Lizzy thought. Tomm tore out after her, but before he could stop her, Goody had bridled and saddled Snap, still screaming a hail of her strange nastiness. Tomm went after her on another horse, but Snap was faster and put a ways between them. She was headed in the direction of McBee's.

Lizzy was alarmed for her mistress's safety, and the baby's. Sick already, Goody was wild and beside herself. Still, Lizzy was relieved to be left alone, with no questions or accusations to answer. There was nothing she could do about her mistress's danger. There was nothing to do but cook and prepare the Red Dog for the day and night ahead. After all, she was training to be a taverner. How well could she do by herself? It would be an adventure.

Hermann

Lizzy knew where there was a big patch of plantain, with young tender leaves and also larger ones that would have to cook a while. The pokeweed Goody loved seemed endless from being cut back so often. The greens could cook all day to be rich and tender. Tomm had bought a supply of strong cheese and a cask of dry maccarony, and there were eggs aplenty. Greens and maccarony cheese! She could have that ready this evening, right soon after noon, and it would last into the night for supper. Corncakes of meal, water, and salt would make the greens-eaters smile, and she had plenty of bear grease for frying them. Travelers stopping in the morning or noon could have the boiled eggs and bacon she usually had on hand, with toasted bread from yesterday. The dough for raised bread she had started before milking would come in good tomorrow! In the back of her mind, Lizzy knew this frenzy of cooking would help her not worry overmuch about Goody or 'Ro and Ahmee. But who would take care of travelers' horses with 'Ro gone? Lizzy could not serve food and take care of horses too. The travelers would just have to feed and rub down their own horses, that's all. She would do this thing, and at least Tomm would be pleased.

Lizzy had helped Goody make maccarony cheese only once, back before she took to her bed. It was too hot to heat all that water for maccarony in the kitchen, so she built a fire at the washing place and filled the biggest wash pot with water. That was work 'Ro used to do, and it took longer than she thought.

While the water heated, she worked up the cheese, grating it and mixing it with eggs in the big stone mortar. She worked in persimmon beer until the cheese sauce was juicy, and last of all she took down some dried red peppers from the wreath, ground them fine, and added them. Later, when the maccarony had cooked and she brought it inside in the pewter bowls, she poured the thick cheese sauce over it and kept it warm on the hearth until time to take it to the tavern. Her last touch was to heat the iron salamander in the fire and hold it over the bowls to brown the cheesy top.

It was a hard day, but the food was good. People started coming into the Red Dog in groups about three o'clock that evening and talked more than usual, though not to her. She did not want to say anything about what had happed that morning and hoped there would be few questions. Visitors were used to Tomm coming and going, knowing Goody was frail. The Morgins had not been there for a while, but they came. Lizzy soon realized Ruly was there too. She had gone straight to Goody's bed, then ran puzzled into the Red Dog.

"Thank the Lord you're here. Goody flew off this morning, and Tomm went after her. She was all in a hornet's nest because Cicero is gone. They reckon he's run away. Can you get Clax to take care of the horses? There's a pile of people coming in here." Ruly's mouth stood open, and for once she said nothing.

The cause of the crowd's excitement became clear when three men came in and asked for "the proprietor."

"Mr. Toliver is away at the moment. I can help you." Lizzy deepened her voice a bit to sound more confident. She was glad Ruly was there too.

"We have a petition to His Majesty about the wrong-doing of his officials hereabouts in Carolina. I have a ready friend in Philadelphia who will direct it." The speaker had removed his hat and spoke stiffly. His thick hair was matted and unruly, but his clothing was clean and very plain.

Astonished, Lizzy stammered, "Will you acquaint me first with its meaning?"

"I will, Miss, and to any who would listen."

"Tell me first, Sir. Only me, if you please." She was more herself now.

The men with him nodded, and the speaker began.

'Tis about the ills that were complained of in Granville County some time back, the same high-handed cheating of regular folks that the big men carry on in all these back parts. The legislature is no better, for these cheating men are members or else merchant-partners of them that are. The schoolteacher Simms on Nutbush Creek, a learned and fair man, drew up a paper and read it before crowds at different gatherings in Granville. He explained it plain. Some said they heered their own troubles stated in the schoolman's telling, it was that true. Everywhere it was read out, there were Huzzas. But now, the men he complained against have sued him for libel. He's in jail where the court meets, on the plantation of the main one he accused. There's no justice to come from that. The paper I bring begs the king to order the schoolman free and to tell the governor to enforce the law."

"You say a friend in Philadelphia will get it to the king? How will he do that?"

"He goes to London for the legislature of Pennsylvania. I know him because he is a printer and printed a book for me." Lizzy wondered who this strange man was, who wrote a book and knew an important traveler, but she kept to the subject.

"I will read your paper, Sir, and I thank you. I need to know about the paper the schoolteacher wrote: did it say unlawful things? Have you seen it?"

"Indeed I have. I have copied the better part of it myself and have it here. It speaks of the true laws of England and how they are broken in the backcountry by the very men who are supposed to uphold them. How they take more money than they are entitled to and protect each other on juries in the courts. Anyone here can read it, or I can read it aloud."

Lizzy quickly read the man's paper. He wanted to leave it here two days and nights for men to sign. He and his friends would spend the night. Lizzy saw nothing wrong with what he said, though never had she read a letter to a king before. It was very respectful and plain. She wished Tomm, or even Mr. Marshall, had been here. She told the stranger to do his talking and to spread his writing on the table. She brought pen and ink, as was expected in a tavern. Then she lit candles, as the late sundown turned evening into night.

Many in the crowd seemed to be there waiting for the newcomer. Everyone paid attention while he quickly told about a schoolteacher in Granville County named Simms. Some already knew about Simms's paper and spoke up for it. When men crowded around the table to mark or sign their names, talk started up among them and among the few women who sat in the door nook. Lizzy rushed to serve all the plates and drinks, but she tried to listen for whatever she could learn and hoped she could talk with the women before they left. She knew Mrs. Molly a little, for she sold small beers to Tomm from time to time. It was near time for her wheat beer, he had said.

When Lizzy was near Pa Morgin, she asked him about the stranger, for Ruly's Pa went to all the places where gossip was in the air. "Some say he stirs trouble ever'where he goes," Pa answered. "He got Quakers to taking sides on some of their matters. It be easy to get Quakers to quarrel amongst their selves, and when they get the matter settled, they won't let on they were ever torn up." So the man's plain clothes and hat are part of the Quaker ways, Lizzy thought. "Howesomever, the gathering of Quakers he belonged to dismissed him for making a disruption among them."

Before Lizzy had to move on to another table, another man added, "It not be just his group around the Cane Creek on yon side the Haw River. Bad feelings spread through all them 'Friends,' as they call their selves, in Orange County – plumb up to Eno and down to Deep Creek, all from Hermann's mischief. Word is, Hermann's some kind of fire ball amongst religious folk." Lizzy planned her steps to stay in earshot, for the speaker had more to say. "I've not had his experiences read to me, but them that has say it be a heartfelt story of Hermann's strivings to know the Saviour's ways. There be folks eager to read such, but not me. One way or t'other, tongues be rattling about him, whether he be . . ." Lizzy missed the last part.

Ruly was helping now, that grand girl! She had taken two wooden trays of dirty pewter to the kitchen and brought back the rest of the food. What would Lizzy be doing with all these people without Ruly? And her father! Old Pa Morgin seemed to be playing the proprietor, but it was help. Why not? He had made half the drink sold tonight, and he and Tomm had some understanding between themselves. To keep up with what she served, she carried chits in her pocket, along with sharpened charcoal. At least it would be a good night's credit for Tomm – if she could put it all down. After filling the empty vessels at a table, she would set down her pitcher while writing her chits. If the talk there was about the man called Hermann, she took her time and listened. She was quick to learn that he was well-regarded and that land had something to do with that. She heard snippets of talk where men said they or someone they knew had been able to get a good piece of land at a fair price with Hermann's help. Whether they had bought land from him or benefitted from his paperwork with the land office was not clear, but it sounded like he had made it easier for a lot of men to get land. He had been in the colony off and on for some ten years and made his home on Sandy Creek of Deep River at the Baptist settlement that Mr. Marshall often mentioned. Mr. Marshall must know him.

Only two or three men were drinking Madeira or rum, and they did not stay long. It was too soon in the year to have peach brandy or cider, so men were drinking either Tomm's whiskey, (weakened with faded tea or water) or spruce beer. Like the fruit drinks, brews made from sumac, locust, and ginger had not been brought in because their ingredients were not yet ripe, but the Morgins' spruce beer kept coming year-round. Lizzy poured pitchers throughout the tavern several times before she could slow down and go to the women's nook. They were drinking spruce beer too, but Lizzy had silently left them a pitcher out of view. She returned now to ask if she could bring something else and offered "a right goodly drop of blackberry cordial." There was little left in the cupboard, but she reckoned it would be enough. As she brought it in fresh cups, she said she knew nothing of the stranger with the paper and hoped they could favor her by telling about him. It was understood that their favor would match her favors to them with pitcher and cordial. "The men see justice in the cause of George Simms," she began, "but what do you ladies think of Mr. Hermann, if that is his name? Is a worthy man? Some say he caused trouble among the Quaker folk."

Slowly, a mouth beneath raised eyebrows spoke, "Ye be a right canny gull, Missy." Lizzy wondered if she had been too bold. "Sit yersel' here to shield from listeners." Lizzy hesitated but sat, facing the chair outward to see the room. Nodding importantly, another woman whispered: "It be a fee-male matter." Lizzy said no more.

"He has proved a worthy man for in-comers trying to get land, and he has profited mightily in an honest way. That is how he became important in North Car'liny." The eyebrows were speaking again. "The Quakers' trouble started in the Cane Creek settlement while he was absent on Maryland business, so he did not start it, but there was no division until he came home two year ago. Hermann raked up old coals and blew on them till he had a raging fire and was dismissed by the Quakers for his meddling. I know about this from my husband's sister who turned Quaker when she married one. She lives on the Pee Dee, which is where the girl's family moved when her troubles started."

"Was not the girl the preacher's own daughter?" a third voice whispered.

"Yes, her mother and another preaching woman started Cane Creek Meeting years ago. You know how Quakers are; preachers are more like organizers and message-bearers than bosses. They don't take to bossing. Quakers have to get everybody to agree before they'll do a thing, or at least have nobody to disagree. My husband's sister explained that to me. Being a Presbytern, that was as new to me as having women ministers." Another woman broke in, "Well, there be some

Baptists what have women preachers too, I heered." No one else was as interested in the Baptist women preachers as they were in the Quaker woman preacher's daughter. Lizzy hoped someone would ask, but she would not.

"What did the daughter do?" At least someone besides Lizzy did not know the details.

"According to her and her mother, she did nothing more than spend time with a young man who took advantage of her."

"I heered that before. Hits what they all say."

"There's more to it than that, Esther. The men of Cane Creek Meeting took away the boy's membership for going about saying he had had his way with most of the girls in the settlement."

"Well, maybe he had," Esther replied, "and maybe they appreciated it."

"I don't know about the others, but the preacher's daughter – Charity was her name—she said she had fought him and that he had overcome her, being stronger. That's what she always held to."

"So what happened?"

"The women tried to get Charity to admit she had carnal knowledge of the boy and to repent and apologize, but she bucked them all. Said she had done nothing to apologize for or to seek forgiveness for, that ill had been done to her, not by her. And her mother stuck by her. The others did not. They dismembered her. But that was not what the disruption was about. It came later, after your man Hermann came back and made a fuss."

"Did he take Charity's side and say they had been wrong to remove her from the church?"

"Egad, no, no, no. He lit in after the mother, said she had done wrong in the thing. And it's not a 'church.' Quakers call it a 'Meeting of Friends.' Plain-like."

Lizzy feared she would get confused. By luck the talking woman – it was still the one with the eyebrows, and they were still up – said simply,

"Listen. It's an in-and-out tale. I'll not chase the rabbit all through the briers. I'll pluck him out directly. After the family moved to the meeting at Pee Dee, the mother axed for a certificate of membership from Cane Creek. She had made apology for her own words before they moved, and Cane Creek Meeting had accepted. So Cane Creek gave her the certificate with no bother. Then when Hermann got back, he talked against her and said her apology had been 'insincere.' He had not even been there at the time but kept talking about how she did not deserve a certificate because she had not 'really' apologized."

"Sounds like Popery and the Inquisition to me," someone said.

"Anyway, like I said, I'll pluck the rabbit right out of the briars: the fussing spread until it got to the Western Quarterly Meeting and then the North Car'liny Yearly Meeting, all the Quaker sets in the colony. The Yearly Meeting dis-membered Hermann for creating disruption! And that be codstrewth!"

"So he's not a Quaker anymore?"

"Who knows what's in his heart, and there are those who think he did right, but the Quakers say he's not one of them now."

"He's one of the best-known men in this part of Carolina, on account of his years of help to regular people with land troubles, then his book telling about his spiritual yearnings, and now there are many who think he was right to stand up for what he believed at Cane Creek." It was Molly Strickland who spoke now, for the first time. "With the hardships we face every day from cheating magistrates and all, Hermann is looked on as a leader, like tonight."

The women had not answered Lizzy's question, but they had told her more than she had asked about Mr. Hermann Husband.

The next morning, a man from the McBee place interrupted her milking with the bad news. He was on his way to the Morgins with a message from Tomm: he wanted them to take a wagon to the widow's to bring home the corpses of Goody and the baby.

Trouble

The first taste of freedom was like a dream.

Wa'ro and Ahmee put the raft in the water and made the vines look undisturbed. Until light, they floated on the channel. Wa'ro slept, knowing Ahmee was a good watcher and had slept some. After daylight, they both slept, well-hidden on a bank. Next night, they went further down the Tarr, lively with whispers and the joy of being together. "For Life, Ahmee, for Life." "Truly for Life, my Love," she replied. They said the words again and again, facing a different direction each time. It was a ritual he remembered from before, and it pleased her mightily.

Gaspar had told her to notice the big streams on the left and to get out of the river upstream from the second one before getting to the ford there, lest someone at the ford see them. It was just before daybreak when they realized they were at the ford already. They moved to the right riverbank, where Gaspar had said a road was nearby that they should take to Tarr Burrow. While they tied the raft to tree roots, a man surprised them.

"Who are ye, Blackamoors, and whose are ye?"

Wa'ro calmed himself and brought out his pass, still sealed. He handed it over, saying, "My name is Cicero, Sir, and here is my pass. The girl has one too. Would you kindly tell me your name and place?" He thought it a fair question, and the man did not mind.

"I run the tavern at the ford and watch for travelers in distress." He added, "Or trouble. I am Cooper Donald Forbes, the constable for Squire McNeil."

"You be Toliver's eh? I'll see hers now. He did not look at Ahmee.

While she brought out her pass, Ahmee heard Wa'ro say, "I take care of horses of visitors to Mr. Toliver's tavern, and whatever else he or his wife put me to."

Forbes looked at Ahmee's pass, then at her but said nothing. Wa'ro was glad the man could read.

"Amy is daughter of the Widow McBee's head horseman, Gaspar. You may know of him." He took care to say her name the way the widow did, for Lizzy told him she wrote it that way.

"I see resemblance with the horseman. Your passes are from one Crenshaw. If you don't live at the same place, how did you both come to have passes from the same magistrate?" Forbes turned the paper over carefully and looked suspicious. Wa'ro's scalp prickled.

"Well, Sir, my master was at Mrs. McBee place when he hired me out to travel for her with her girl Amy." He nearly said "Ahmee."

The pass does not state your business, only tells what counties you can travel. What is it you're doing for Mrs. McBee that her own people can't do, and what is the girl's errand?"

Ahmee spoke before Wa'ro could answer. "I have doves here Sir. My mother keeps the dovecote and is training me. Missus entrusted me to deliver them safe to her kinsman, Squire Hogg near Blount's Ford. I have been there with Missus before."

"And I am to bring Mrs. McBee two young horses she has bought from Squire Hogg."

"Two things I don't understand. What is Toliver getting for your hire, and why does the girl have to go, too? You can manage a basket of birds, can't you?"

"Begging your pardon, Sir," Ahmee spoke again. "Doves are an art and a mystery to handle, and I know them well." Forbes looked annoyed by Ahmee's speaking freely. Wa'ro quickly answered him.

"Mr. Toliver, he getting four casks of Madeira for my going, packed on the horses. Squire Hogg buys it from the sea-ships and trades it up the country."

"Where is Blount's Ford, boy? You talk, not her!"

"Across the Roanoke River, Sir, on other side of Tarr Burrow. We be going through Tarr Burrow and expect our passes to help us get through." Wa'ro would feel better with the passes returned to them, but Constable Forbes made no move.

"Never mind Tarr Burrow. Folks there not alert enough to question ye. Ye'll see more trouble on the road-paths with scoundrels coming and going than in the village. Are ye headed to the road now, or do you mean to stay on the river until Tarr Burrow?" Wa'ro thought the road would be safer, now that they were where people were getting thicker on the river. Gaspar had told Ahmee they should get off the river here because it got more crooked before Tarr Burrow, and the bends would take more time than the road. Wa'ro wondered which way the man thought was best. Even people with passes could get kidnapped, and every time somebody questioned them, it would take up their time, like now. They were impatient to get on but dared not show it.

While the constable stalled, Wa'ro's mind raced through the other story he had in mind if people doubted the need for Ahmee to go. He had not told her because it pained him, but he would use the lie if he had to.

"Strange to me that neither owner signed the pass. The Widow McBee has her letters and more, and Toliver could at least make his mark. This is not the usual way, boy. Mayhap I should tek ye to the squire."

"Sir, may I speak alone, please?" This was for show, but he didn't want Ahmee to hear it anyway. He would tell her after they were safe. They stepped away from Ahmee, and Wa'ro turned his back to her and spoke confidentially to Forbes. He had to get this right, or they would fail on the spot.

"The girl does not know, but she to be sold at Squire Hogg's. She the price of the horses and wine. The passes did not say that, for she would hear them read. She travels easy not knowing, or she might slip away from me."

"That makes more sense." Forbes seemed relieved with his puzzle solved. "Go on, the two of you. There be vittles at the tavern. You are welcome if you can pay."

"We brought our own. We'll eat here in the shade."

Worse Trouble

After Forbes walked away, Wa'ro sank to the ground, drained from the scare. They were hungry, and the pone soon filled them. "What did you say to him?" she asked.

Wa'ro laughed, relaxing at last, and pulled her to him. "Nothing much, my sweet, nothing much." She swatted at him, pretending to pout.

A sickening voice from within a clump of alders made their skin crawl.

"Well, well, Tomm Toliver's Neeg, a long way from the Red Dog, ain't cha?" As they jumped up, a skinny man grabbed Ahmee around the waist and flashed a knife at her throat. Beads of her blood stood like sumac seeds on the knife edge. "Be a shame to kill a valuable Negress. I'd do it, though, or at least scar up this comely face fer the chance of selling yer own black self, ye high an' mighty Cee-ce-roo! Ne'er thought y'e fall into the hands of Snake Travers, did ye? Ye 'n 'at white wench o' Toliver's innerferin' w' my trading, wearin' down my profit."

Wa'ro stood stock-still so as to not rile Travers. There was no sign of Buckhorn. Did the trader still have him? The wagon was not in sight; maybe Travers left Buckhorn to guard it. "What you aim to do with us, Mr. Travers?"

"Git as much money fer ye as I can, that's what. I can sell ye both at New Hanover Courthouse before any notice is in the paper and in time to skedaddle. I know ye runned away. Yer passes didn't fool me. And, he looked hard at Wa'ro, I heered everything. All o' it."

His words struck deep in Ahmee. She side-kicked the man, pushing her head against his chest as far back from the knife as she could. Her right hand pushed against the forearm that held it, far enough to sink her teeth in the underside of his arm.

Seeing her move, Wa'ro grabbed Travers's long hair, still tied behind his neck, and hollered, "Buck! Buckhorn! It's Ro! Ro! Help!" Wa'ro twisted the hair around his own fist. Still calling for Buck, who might not even be there, Wa'ro pushed the traders' neck toward the blade till he made him drop the knife. Travers still held Ahmee tight by the waist with his left hand, and she was bent over. She had pulled her horn knife from her right legging. She knew Travers could take it from her with his right hand, so she sliced straight up his right leg and threw the knife towards Wa'ro. Travers was not wearing chaps in the summer heat, and he was a good bleeder.

Wa'ro's mind raced while he grappled with the trader. There was rope on the raft, but even if they tied him up, what could they do with him? If they left him, he would only report them as runaways, and they would be caught. They could report him first! They knew where the constable was. They could tell how he attacked them and said he would sell them quickly. Travers would rail against the passes, but he had been the offender, and the passes looked good. It might seem like they were in the right. No: the constable would send to Tomm or the widow!! Not that!

Ahmee had taken Travers' knife to the raft and brought back rope. She and Wa'ro were struggling to tie the trader up when Buckhorn came tearing through the undergrowth. Buck carried a long iron tool, the hub chisel with a heavy end that Travers kept in the wagon, and he knocked Travers out with a single blow. He knew where to hit, Ahmee thought. She had never seen either of them and did not know their past. Wa'ro, who did, thought his friend must have planned that blow for a long time and took this chance to use it.

They all wondered if the trader were dead.

"He's sure to be found, alive or dead," Wa'ro whispered. "And questions raised, unless – unless a gator gets to him, smelling blood."

What a notion! Wa'ro and Ahmee looked at each other, but Buckhorn, wordless so far, spoke up: "I know better way." Then, slapping Wa'ro on the arm as a greeting, "Stay with him. I'll raft off to find a good place, not take long."

They sat silently on either side of Travers, who was tied hands and feet and still not moving. He could be playing possum, so their eyes swept from him to the river and back toward the unseen path. Buckhorn returned, a hard look frozen on his face. Whoever this boy was, Ahmee was glad he was Wa'ro's friend.

"Take things off the raft. Girl, stay here with things. We'll pole him on the raft up to where I found a stretch of *shoshu* -- viper moccasins." Wa'ro did not understand, but Ahmee did.

She shivered. "Poison, like copper snakes and rattlers, but they live in water like the little water snakes where we live, that have no poison. Here, the big white mouths kill quick. It is good. He will never know."

A little upstream, Wa'ro saw the cottonmouths. It shocked him to see how closely he and Ahmee had floated past them feeding on insects in a swampy by-water. Their muscular bodies were longer than the water snakes he had seen, and you could see their whole bodies, not just the heads that showed on water snakes. There were so many! Buckhorn told him they should untie Travers so it would look like an accident if someone found his body. They needed to put him at a corner of the raft, then get out on the bank and use the pole to push the raft into the snakes. Wa'ro did everything as Buck said. Then they sat briefly on the bank, watching the ghastly thing they had made happen. When the raft rushed into the snakes' space, they struck at it and at every part of Travers they could get to, even swarming onto the raft. It bumped the bank and tossed the body over the edge, where a frenzy of thrashing bodies and gaping mouths ensured death. Even Buckhorn was overcome: "Worst thing ever I see." Wa'ro had seen worse, but what he was looking at now brought a rush of sourness up his throat, and the cornpone left him.

Ahmee was holding their clothes and food, and she quickly walked beside Wa'ro as Buckhorn led them to the wagon and horses that had belonged to Travers. "These horses know me," he assured them. "Where you going on raft? I can take you. If you runaway, I can be runaway with you. I cannot go home before two springs."

"Go with us." Wa'ro grinned. "This is Ahmee. We jumped the creek." Turning to her, "Buckhorn is my friend, from when he and the man brought skins to Toliver."

Buckhorn was puzzled. "You jump across creek? Many creeks here, Brother. What creek you jump?"

Wa'ro smiled and touched Ahmee. "That means we decided to be together always, and we made promises. Like jumping from old life alone to new life together."

Buckhorn closed his eyes and smiled. "Good words. Good man. Good woman. You have good feel. Buckhorn have good feel for you. Sister." He reached across Wa'ro to place his fingers gently on Ahmee's.

She wanted to know about the dead man. "Thank you for helping us. Who was the man, and why did you hate him so?"

"Trader, bought deerskins from my family, cheated us big. Took me to work for him long time. Name Travers. Snake Travers."

They laughed so hard they farted.

Beyond Tarr Burrow

On the road, Buckhorn drove confidently, as he was accustomed to Travers' lying on the skins, asleep or drinking. Wa'ro sat next to Buck, and their easy conversation helped Wa'ro look natural when they were near other travelers. Ahmee was less sure, and she knew it. She knew also that her looks attracted men's attention. Besides, two black bodies with an Indian would raise more questions than just one black body would. She hid under the skins, and the other two were glad. They would need her directions when they reached Tarr Burrow, but by that time it would be dark.

The elements were good to them that night, with a clear sky and low water. Tarr Burrow village was small, no more than fifty houses, they guessed, and they could see clearly to move straight through it to the Tarr River. They crossed it at a ford upstream from a ferry, and it was not hard to pick the road Gaspar had told them about on the other side. It skirted the river. They saw little sign of travelers but smelled fires from a few camps. All three were practiced hands with horses, and they took turns driving and sleeping. They stopped before light, for several streams joined the river, and they did not want to miss the one Gaspar had told Ahmee to follow into the high swamp that was their destination.

The stream led directly into the swamp, further than the wagon could go. Sensing that they would be found, they stayed with the wagon, fed and watered the horses, ate, and waited. Before the sun brought its full heat, two women came and led them along a hidden cart way to a clearing. For the rest of the day, they answered questions, at first one at a time. They held back nothing they were asked. All the skills they said they had were useful, and the people said they could stay there until early spring, a proving time. Then, if all agreed, they could live there. They called their place Conneta Swamp and said it was a "pock-oh-sin." Buckhorn had heard the word before, but Wa'ro and Ahmee had not.

The next morning, Ahmee took a small square of linen and with a burnt stick drew on it two birds. She tied it to the leg of one of her doves and released it.

That evening, Minerva unwrapped the linen and rejoiced.

The House of Death

At the Red Dog, Lizzy and Ruly could not think straight-on about the awful thing that had happened with Goody and the baby, so they thought on it around the edges, letting their hands do work that had to be done. Ruly never thought of leaving her friend by herself to get ready for what the burial day would bring. They found some cloth to drape over the sign of the Red Dog to show it was closed. There would be folks enough crowding in tomorrow. Word always spread fast, so neighbors would know not to come to the Red Dog today. If any travelers happened through, well, they could just keep traveling. The girls had to have all day to get the place ready, and they would cook for tomorrow into the night. Following her habit, Lizzy made raised bread. She made twice her usual amount, enough for the people who would pay their respects this evening and for the next day too, the burial day, and she made cornpone as well. Usually with a death, some people would spend the night. She was glad she had the rooms ready; Goody had taught her to keep them that way.

Scrubbing floors, tables, porches, and all the woodwork they could reach put a little cushion between them and the horror they had to face. Different thoughts rushed through Lizzy's mind. Goody – the peculiar, hard-to-please woman who had shaped Lizzy's days since Mother died – was no more. With Wa'ro gone, now it would be just Tomm and Lizzy to run the Red Dog and do all the work. Lizzy felt ashamed of herself for thinking right off about the work that would fall to her! Anyhow, Goody had done so little work lately, and truth to tell, she had been lazy ever since Lizzy came. The strange woman had some softness about her heart, though, and she told rattling good stories. Once or twice, the girl had felt a little like family with Goody and Tomm. Lizzy felt that loss.

Mainly she felt for poor Tomm. He was besotted with Goody, with all her petty ways and face paints. And on top of that, the baby! Such loss might change Tomm. What would he be like to work for now? Goody always had been there, to tell Lizzy what to do. Could Lizzy think about all to be done, and plan ahead, without Goody on hand? Well, she thought, I am here to learn what the court called "the art and mystery of" tavern keeping. That's what they said about all apprenticeships -- to learn "the art and mystery of" whatever they were set to do: farming, mantua-making, keeping house, repairing wagons, everything that grown-ups needed done. Guess that's how you learn how to be a grown-up, she reckoned. It was more than a body getting bigger and changing. She had never thought about it that way.

Neither girl spoke for a long while, each thinking her own thoughts. All at once, Ruly blurted out a notion that had been pestering her mind. "I could have kept her from dying," she wailed. Before Lizzy could ask, Ruly went on. "I suspicioned she was doing herself harm. She kept on using those medicinals she said helped her get with child, like they would help her keep it. I did not know enough to argue, but she was keeping it from Miz Minerva. Oh, Lord, Lord," she bawled. "I shoulda told Miz

Minerva my own self. Mayhaps them extra yarbs pizzened Miz Goody. And there was a sign, Lizzy, a sign, but I disregarded it! Me, who suspicioned she was hurting herself!

"What sign?" Lizzy did not know much about the "signs" people talked about, more than the moon's signs telling when to plant and sow. Ruly meant warning signs, omens. Ruly's face looked frozen.

"A death forecast: the ember of death, when a hearth fire spits out an ember shaped just like a coffin! It means someone in that house will die soon. The fire knows!"

The awfulness of it cut Lizzy's heart, but she did not want her friend to feel worse than she already did. It made sense to Lizzy now, how Goody had weakened so fast and looked sicker and sicker every day. It could be from the extra medicinals. Goody likely poisoned her own self without knowing! Lizzy did not say this; Ruly was thinking it already.

Instead, Lizzy said, "I heered my mother say to other women, "When a coming baby has something wrong, there is no way to make it right, and the mother or baby is likely to die." She let her friend hear that, because she had told Ruly so many times about Mother's wisdom. Not having her own mother, Ruly put great stock in things Lizzy told about Mother. Lizzy looked straight at her friend and went on, "Ruly, you did not see the state Goody was in when she tore out of here yesterday. She had not been out of the bed for weeks, or wore regular clothes. When Tomm told her about 'Ro being gone, she moved like lightening, wearing no more than a shift, with her hair loose, and without bite or swallow. She was plumb out of her head, a wild, raging creature. I tell you, Ruly, in my heart I knew she was not long for this world. I could not say it to myself until this minute, but I knew. As hard as it is to say, and I'll not say it beyond you, but Goody killed herself from taking too much medicinals. Now, that's said between us. Tomm and other folks can realize for themselves, or not. We know."

It was quite a speech Lizzy had said, but she thought it was needed. For the rest of the scrubbing, they held their separate thoughts, but they were more calm. Sometimes, Lizzy's mind flew to Wa'ro and Ahmee, wondering how far they had got. She longed to confide in Rudy about them, but that was way too dangerous to speak of, even to a trusted friend. Some things are best kept to yourself.

Early in their scrubbing, the girls stopped to lay wood for a fire under the wash pot and fill it with water. They started a bigger fire some distance away. Lizzy was not sure what they would cook for tomorrow's crowd, but for sure they would need hot water and plenty of coals for cooking out of doors. She kept thinking through what-all they had that could feed a crowd without using up their hardest to get supplies. She reckoned the neighbors would come in this evening with food to be cooked for the burial day, like folks generally did. Beans and corn were still growing in some fields. She had a feeling she would make some kind of savory stew with whatever was brought. There was plenty of salted pork that could be cut up and put in the pot to start the savory when it got to boiling, but it would take several hours for the wood to make coals for good cooking. No coffin embers, please, she thought towards the fire. She didn't know if she believed that sign, but if Ruly did, fine; maybe she wouldn't blame herself if she thought death had been coming to the house anyway.

It was usual for people to "sit up with the dead" the night before the burying. It was a matter of respect, but also there was a notion that the body might not be dead, and if it stirred or showed any sign of life, someone should be there to know. To bury a person alive was a dread fear. The girls expected the visiting to be this evening and tonight and the burial tomorrow morning, so a few people would sit up tonight. If it were winter, there wouldn't be a hurry, but in this late summery weather, heat could make it unpleasant.

They talked these plans through while they cut tete greens from the garden patch. There was plenty of okro as well, but it would be best cut tomorrow morning. Lizzy had not known tete until Minerva brought seeds, saying the leaves would be nourishing for Goody. Wa'ro had known the plant from Africa, and he sowed it. As soon as the girls got the pork going, they gathered all the extra vessels they had, filled them with water, and put them in the tavern, ready for the rosemary they cut and put in them. It was good they had plenty. In fact, when someone died, Goody always went to the house early with a load of the sweet-smelling herb. She grew more rosemary than anyone, on account of the cooking. The girls brought more rosemary than they had vessels for, piling it in clumps throughout the tavern. They pushed the best table to the center and banked it with rosemary. Now the big room was ready for the sad arrival of its landlady in her coffin, her poor arms around a tiny baby.

No sooner had they placed the last rosemary clumps when several people showed up in a wagon piled with vittles and cooking vessels. Lizzy was mighty glad to see this; now she could plan what to cook, and the extra vessels would come in good. Old Zack Henley drove the wagon, and he was the one who brought meat that Lizzy would plan the food around. That much at least Lizzy could see her way through.

"Ah, Gull, 'tis a sad time," he nodded to Lizzy. "Least I could do was go out and do my best to get a hearty deer for my friend Tomm Toliver to entertain the mourners of his good wife." The women in the wagon took her and Ruly by the hands and murmured a few words. They carried baskets of cheese and unpeeled boiled eggs. Then they got down onions, garlic, leeks, potatoes, fennel and bunches of other herbs, all clean and ready to be cut up. Lizzy thanked them deeply, glad they would not have to wash everything before peeling and cutting. That could be done late this night or early morrow. She could get the meat ready and cook it overnight, then put in the other things, and a fine venison stew would last the coming day.

While the women carried their offerings into the kitchen, Ruly ran out to meet Molly Strickland. She had brought new-made crabapple cider and young locust pods. Molly made beer from locusts after they ripened, but the green pods with young seeds were good to eat. Ruly thought they would be extra good mixed with the tete greens. "Your presence will be a comfort to

Lizzy, Miz Molly," Ruly smiled, knowing her friend admired the woman.

Not knowing when Tomm and the Morgins would reach the Red Dog with the bodies of Tomm's family, Lizzy and Ruly were anxious to have a supper spread for him and his guests. The women helped fill platters with the eggs, cheese, and bread, and took them to the tavern. Ruly and Lizzy brought in the tete and locusts they had cooked quickly in the hot pork-seasoned water, and Molly had her cider at the ready, assuring the growing crowd that it was "new" cider, not much fermented yet, and "proper for all manner of drinkers, from chil'ren to oldsters." The good appearance of the supper and the comfortable manner of the visitors showing their respect calmed Lizzy. She no longer dreaded seeing Tomm, and the thought surprised and comforted her. She and Ruly washed their hands and faces and put on clean aprons. They mingled through the groups of people, careful to stay between the spread tables and a few men whose impatient eyes kept darting toward them. Molly, standing by the cider barrel, was a perfect guardian of dignity. Whisperers wondered if "airy a preacher" was close enough to be with Tomm and conduct a funeral. It was a good question, but Lizzy knew that if it were at all possible, Mr. Marshall would be here.

Sunilda, the Lost Daughter

It was getting toward twilight when the Morgin's largest wagon arrived. Someone had draped the horses' harnesses with black cloth. The driver was not Pa Morgin, but Gaspar McBee. Tomm sat behind him, next to Mr. Marshall, who held a bundle, and the coffin rode behind them. A short ways beyond, a smaller wagon approached. The Morgin men rode in it, along with a young woman holding a small child. There was a big basket at her feet. Zack motioned for Lizzy to walk beside him, as he led the men outside to greet the procession. What a mercy she had changed her apron! The women rose, and two or three began keening in low tones. As soon as the men reached the wagon, they lifted the coffin. Tomm and Mr. Marshall followed it into the tavern, and the men placed it on the center table. Standing beside Tomm at the head of the coffin, Mr. Marshall placed his bundle in Tomm's arm. Disturbed, the bundle let out a wail. Tomm unwrapped a corner, revealing a face and head the size and color of a pink apple. "Friends," Tomm struggled to speak, "Some part of my dear Goody still lives. I have here our daughter Sunildy, the Lord God's own miracle."

Amidst the gasps and shuffling, Lizzy moved away from the crowd, knowing it was up to her to make the visitors comfortable with food and drink and that she should not block anyone's view or hearing of Tomm and the baby. She was as amazed as anyone, but she knew she would get the details soon. Ruly pushed ahead, as was her way, and boldly took a place near Tomm, grasping his hand for an instance and listening close. When she turned back toward Lizzy, Ruly's eyes were shooting their yellow sparks, and her words rushed out: "Minerva! Miz Minerva saved that baby! She never gave her up for dead but took her aside while the others were moaning and praying. Tomm said she rubbed the baby with warm cloths and yarbs for ever so long before any part of her twitched, and all that time Tomm thought the baby was dead. Tomm's got a baby, Lizzy, a real baby! Born before her time, but alive! And Elke Tikell has come as wet-nurse. She still nurses her child, so her milk runs yet." As she spoke, Ruly caught the eye of the young woman who had been in the Morgin's wagon. Lizzy recognized her now, from court, where the little dark boy with her had been apprenticed to the widow McBee! He looked to be near-about two now. Benjamin. His mother had called his name in court, Lizzy remembered. Elke Tikell responded to Ruly's look. She left the boy with a woman, took a deep breath, and crossed the room toward Lizzy and Ruly.

Nodding slightly to Lizzy, Elke said, "My condol'ses, Missy. I offered Mr. Tomm my services for the babe, and ye'll be needing some help with the Red Dog, I dare say. I am to stay until Sunilda is weaned. She has started to take the breast, and there is plenty milk for her and my own. While they are peaceable, I can start helping you get food ready for tomorrow." Ruly seemed suspicious, but Lizzy grasped Elke's hand in relief.

"Here come the Lincolns. They'll be good help." Ruly smiled as Cinda, the one Jackson Morgin was sweet on, led her sisters toward Lizzy. Their father stopped to talk with Tomm. Cinda Lincoln knew Lizzy was only a servant at the Red Dog. She spoke to Ruly, then turned to Lizzy like a lady taking charge.

"Lizzy, we have brought more crockery as a gift to Mr. Toliver for this occasion. Between my sisters and me, we can keep the serving table supplied with food and clean ware from the kitchen. You can go back there and attend to the doings for the morrow. I see Mrs. Strickland already has charge of the libations. Good. My family intends to stay the night and do what is needful for poor Mr. Toliver."

"Thank you, Misses Lincoln," Lizzy held her head high as she looked at all three, a trifle annoyed by Cinda's manner. "I may be a servant," she thought, "but as of tonight, I am the woman of the house." Silently, she chided herself, knowing the big stew would need hours to make, even with Ruly and Elke helping her. It was good to have the Lincoln girls mind the table. Two women who had come with Zack were in the kitchen, finding useful things to do. Lizzy explained to them what she intended to serve the next day and laid out the steps for making the stew. Of course, she knew the women knew how to make venison stew, but Lizzy thought Goody would want her apprentice to direct matters in Goody's own kitchen. The women seemed relieved. They were not used to cooking for a tavern full of folks.

Lizzy chose the hardest job for herself, Ruly, and Elke – cutting the meat into equal sized chunks, rolling it in flour with salt and dried herbs, then taking it outside to brown in skillets over the coals. After they browned it, they would cook it in the pot of pork water from which she had lifted the tete greens earlier. All that flavor would be good. The pot would cook all night over low coals without boiling, so it would be as tender as possible. The women were cutting the other things and would put them in with the meat after it had cooked a while.

Ruly was glad they had Elke to themselves. There were things she wanted to know about her. Maybe Lizzy would ask some of them, and Ruly would not seem so nosy, but Ruly was determined to find out. As they talked, it dawned on Lizzy that Ruly might think Elke wanted Tomm. What nonsense.

The main thing Ruly wanted to know was whether Elke was married or paired off with a man. Lizzy opened that door for Ruly's curiosity by asking Elke how "little Benjamin" was getting on, a friendly enough question. It seemed easy to talk while they cut the meat and rolled it in the flour and seasonings.

"The folk at Mc Bee's are good to him. The widow lets me live there and give him my milk still, and I work for her."

"That is beautiful," Lizzy murmured. "The court sent me here the same day they sent Benjamin to Mrs. McBee. I have wondered how he fared."

"The best part is now he has a daddy," Elke smiled. The girls stared.

"My husband is a trading man. He comes to the McBee place on his rounds. He is good to us. Benjamin already is saying "Dada.""

"What manner of man is he?" Ruly was curious about a traveling man who would marry a woman with a base-born child.

"My husband is of the Crying Bird band. They live among the Occaneechi, near the Oenock River. His name is Fisher Crying Bird."

The word Occaneechi started Lizzy, and she was glad Ruly continued: "We know an Occaneechi boy, name of Buckhorn. Came through here late winter working for a deerskin man."

"The trader's name was Travers." Lizzy wondered if Elke would know either name. She did.

"I heered tell of Travers. Did he trade here?" She sounded careful. Lizzy was careful too: "Not exactly like he wanted to." Maybe that would get more out of Elke.

"I don't know him, but Fisher says he has a name of cheating people. He mostly sells whiskey in Fisher's homeland, in exchange for skins the people save for trade. Fisher sells different things, but he does not sell whiskey. He says it's safer that way. He takes skins for trade, and also things people make."

"Does Fisher trade at Big Jeff Osborne's?"

"I think everybody trades at Osbornes, but mostly Fisher trades to the west of here. He goes from settlement to settlement, buying and selling whatever folk want to swap, if he can carry it on his packhorses. He can peddle in places wagons can't get to."

After some silence, Ruly blurted, "So, how did you meet him, and how did you come to marry?" adding, "Not meaning to be nosy, but yours is an interesting case."

Elke's Story

Lizzy heard the question as she toted two more carrying trays to hold the meat. She figured Elke was used to people wanting to know all her business.

The prying did not bother Elke. "I knew Fisher long before I left my home. He traded in our settlement from time to time."

"Did you live anywheres near here?"

"Oh, no. I lived on Tikell Creek, away on the west side of the Haw River. Ours is the northernest of the German settlements on that part of the river. If you know of Pinson's Mill or the High Rock or the Reedy Fork, that is the area." The girls did not.

"Fisher knew interesting things. Not just the news from where he had just come from, which the menfolk always expected. Fisher said his grandfather knew the Ossipee people that used to be thick along the rivers and creeks where we lived. And his elders had told him about how some of the Occaneechi people had moved from the north to the Oenock and other places a good while ago. I liked to hear that, and Fisher always had something I liked hearing. I looked forward to his trading days."

"But, how . . . ?"

"How did we meet after I went into fosterage?"

"What's fosterage?"

"Do your people not do it? It is when a family agrees with another family to take a child who is up in years and train that child in useful ways. Two families might take each other's children. Always the families in different settlements, so the young people learn new people and more of the world than they would learn at home. Sometimes the families may be a little kin, but not much, because they don't want inbreeding. It is not unusual for a fostered person to find a mate in the new place, usually with a neighbor of their foster family." She smiled and continued, "It is thought that young people will pay attention and learn more from another family than from their own family, whose ways and trifles they are used to."

"I heered of people doing that in olden days, I have." Ruly surprised herself. "It maybe was like training a young horse that was getting its head. Boys and girls could learn to control themselves so they wouldn't get in trouble when they got out on their own."

Elke laughed in agreement. "Parents could choose according to what the foster parents knew how to do well. Fosterage is supposed to improve the child's life."

"Do you think it does?" Lizzy had to ask.

"Usually. Often it makes little difference. The children mostly work as servants. They generally come home in a better temper than they left and respect their parents more. And they are able to move out and support themselves. There are many jobs for servants and laborers, and the people who hire them want them well-trained. Fosterage comes at a trying time, when a boy or girl needs to finish growing up."

"What did you learn?" Ruly had to know.

"Well, I learned new weaving patterns and had a baby. Seems I disgraced everyone."

Lizzy wondered if Elke meant to tell this much. "Did you foster in Johnston County?" It seemed a polite question.

"I did. My parents wanted me to foster in one of the Moravian towns. Katrina, one of our neighbors, had good luck as a house servant in Salem. Not just luck. She is a hard worker and won the respect of people there. She married the young man who was hired as the town's farm manager. He went there soon after she did. Everyone knew he needed a wife's help, and Katrina was first choice. Now most of the young people want to foster there."

"But not you?"

"Truly, I admire much about the Moravians. But they are people with set ways of doing things. Fair rules, I think, but I did not think I had the temper for it. So my parents sent me in the other direction and chose a family near here! I suspicioned they were punishing me by sending me so far from them. My foster family are Swiss Germans and started out in Halifax County, but now brothers have farms in Johnston County and moved their slave people here from Halifax. I was in charge of making clothes for them, and I helped with weaving. I liked the work. But you axed me how I met Fisher after I left home." Elke was moving away from the interesting subject of her baby. Lizzy thought that was fair. Ruly was vexed.

"That Fisher, he came looking for me when I was not home at his next visit. Instead of entertaining someone else with his talk, he axed where I was. It took him a while to find me, because that was about when Bentjamin was born. They let me stay where I was till I birthed him, and I named him for the old man of the family for his kindness. But there was the Johnston County Court with a case ready against me when the January term opened. I think my name was first on the list for bastardy cases."

"So your man Fisher found you before or after you went to the widow's?"

"Right soon after. My foster family told him what happened. Fisher brings iron to Mrs. McBee's blacksmith from an ironworks in Orange County, so next time he came to the

McBee place, he inquired for me. It didn't bother him none about Bentjamin. He stayed at the widow's two-three days, living with Gaspar's family in the quarters. Right before Fisher left, he sounded me out and told me to think it through. He would come back in a week specially to know if I was agreeable. Then he'd talk to the widow and we'd figure how to marry. He knew I could not leave Benjamin, so Fisher and I could be together only when he was close by. So that's what we did."

Lizzy was the nosy one now. "But could you really get married? I heered talk that by the law, only Church of England ministers cam marry people up, and I never seed one of them in my life. Seems like folks just get their own preachers to marry them anyway whenever a preacher passes through a settlement. I heered preachers keep a record of who they marry, just like the Church of England does. Is that how you were married?"

"That's right. The widow's a Presbyterin, and all her kin. She allus knows all their doings, and she sent out word she wanted a minister to come if airy a one was nigh. Truth to tell, she talked to me about Fisher the day after he left, so Fisher must have sounded *her* out too. There was a Mr. Criswell came to visit 'Sister McBee' the same day Fisher came back to learn my mind! He was a minister, so he married us then and there."

Ruly snorted, "That'us no happenstance! How come the widow was so accommodating? You're a servant, ain'tcha? And your husband's a pack-horse trader, not some big merchant! She's got control of your son, so it's not like you're a-gone fly off. Why'us she so good to y'all?

"I don't know the widow's mind, but she's always studying folks, high and low. It's a good deal of coming and going at her place. She minds all of them, quiet like. Widow McBee has a name for being canny, so she might reckon some good will come to her someday because we're married." Elke said nothing for a few seconds, then, "one thing is come of it already. We're bound to her closer."

Ruly's grunt meant she understood. Her cleaver went down hard again on the chunk of deer meat she was handling. Being a canny creature herself, and one who pays attention, she found no surprise in the widow's help. Lizzy, however, had even more reason to admire Mrs. McBee. A twinge of guilt reminded her of her own role in depriving that lady of Ahmee.

Elke's Unexpected Story

Elke went on, "Mrs. McBee and the preacher were firm in holding that our being man and wife together was as good in the sight of the Almighty as the marriage of them that might someday take advantage of us because of who married us. And we saw Mr. Criswell write our names under the last couples he had married, in the Hawfields the Sunday before. Why, my own kin on the west side of the Haw River know some of the Irish on the east side, though they don't see much of each other. Our names are in the same book now, even if it's not a law book.

Are your people Presbyterian?" Lizzy wanted to know.

"No, but close. They were Reformed Church people in Germany and kept to their ways when they came over to Pennsylvany, and they still do to this day. They have meeting places in all their settlements, like the Irish do in theirs. The Irish don't know German, and most Germans don't know English. We keep to our own, but everybody where I was raised knows that our beliefs and church do-in's came from the old-time Reformer Jean Calvin, same as the Presbyterin's. They call him John Calvin, and the Baptists do too. Also, the French Protestants around and about and all the way down to Charles Town got their church ways and prayers from the preaching of Herr Calvin and books he wrote. He was a sharpish, smart man and understood Scripture, my people say. So, I was glad to be married by a Presbyterin and have my Bentjamin baptized by him. Fisher knew more about the church thinking than I thought he would, and he had a long talk with the preacher, just them two, and he got baptized, too. Fisher said something curious, that since he liked the butter, he wanted the whole cow, or summot like that. Anyhow, we're rightful Presbyterins."

They were almost finished rolling the meat chunks and loading them on trays to take outside. Other women were spreading coals out from the fire and setting iron trivets on them to heat up. Greased iron skillets were ready to set on the trivets. As the girls and Elke were finishing, Ruly turned to Elke. She spoke more slowly than usual.

"There's a mighty puzzle in what you said. I am not a scholar, and I want to know how your Calvin man got about to all them places you spoke. You said your Reform people in Germany learned from him, and also Presbyterins in Ireland and some sort in France too, all before any o'them come over here to Ameriky. Be them places close by one another?"

Elke thought hard and spoke with care. "First off, Herr Calvin was French, but when France took to warring within itself, he moved to Switzerland where he could be safe. Switzerland is next to France, but much smaller. It's also next to lands where people speak our kind of German – Allemanish-- like Swabia, Alsace, and Baden way up the Rhine River. Herr Calvin moved to Switzerland about 200 years ago, before there were many white people in America, excusing the Spanish people who had moved in way, way south of here."

Elke waited for this to soak in. "Calvin already was a learned man, a priest, and a teacher," she went on. "Switzerland did not have a king. Local groups of men did all the ruling. That made it easier for Calvin to pick a place where he and his followers would not be bothered. They were trying to get people to change some of the ways of the church. They did this by studying, preaching, writing books, and talking. Priests who liked what Calvin was doing in Switzerland went there from many countries and helped." Elke thought she might be losing Ruly's attention, talking about places the girl did not know. She tried to think how to make it plainer, but Ruly spoke suddenly:

"Is that how Calvin's thinking got to all those countries, Ireland and all? Was it by those men going home and preaching what Calvin had taught?"

Ruly's fast thinking shocked Elke. It did not surprise Lizzy, who needed a few more seconds to catch the meaning of Ruly's words.

Elke smiled and let out her breath. "Brave girl! That's the tasty nut in the shell! One bit more, though, if you want to get all the way to the Irish Presbyterins in these parts." Both girls harkened. Mother had told Lizzy some of what Elke was telling, but Elke seemed to know the whole big story and how it all fit together! How things that had happened across the ocean made things the way they were now in Carolina!

"One of Herr Calvin's followers was an Englishman, name of John Knox. He went among the Calvin men in Switzerland when the queen of England was a lady of the old church, the Catholic Church. Queen Mary she was, and she wanted to rid her country of all of the changers, or 'Protestants,' as they were being called. So a lot of English priests, not just Knox, left home while Mary was queen, and they studied under Calvin and his crowd. When Mary died, they all went back to England and kicked up a fuss to make the Church of England become more like churches in other countries that were following the ways of either Calvin or Martin Luther, a German Protestant."

Ruly and Elke set down the heavy tray of rolled meat they had carried outside to the table near the fire. Lizzy had finished loading the last of the trays. She opened and closed the door for them, listening to every word. Relieved of the tray's weight, Elke caught her breath a moment.

"Then what happened?"

"The English Protestants got some of what they wanted: the Church of England was turning Protestant fast at that time. But it kept bishops, like it had all those centuries ago when it had been Catholic. The difference was that the Pope had no say-so over the English bishops anymore. Still, many English Protestants argued against keeping bishops."

Ruly's patience gave out. She had an idea of what a pope was, sort of a king over all the Catholics, she thought. But what in Bee-el-zee-bub was a bishop, and what did it have to do with how Presbyterins got to Car'liny? They were balancing another full tray now, so she kept quiet.

When the tray was on the table, Lizzy rescued her friend's patience.

"What did they have against bishops?"

"Well, Calvin had worked out a way to not have bishops, and it was working. Each church would send a representative, usually its minister, to a council to make decisions for its churches, then *that* council would select its representatives to *another* council to decide bigger questions for more churches, and so on. One name for a council was presbytery, by the by."

"I wondered where that curious name came from."

Ruly still looked puzzled, so Elke took it a step further.

"Look. How do you think this council or 'presbyterin' system would work in a country that has a king?"

Lizzy picked up the question with another one: "Would the king be in any of these councils?"

"If he were elected to one. Or she, if it's a queen."

Ruly followed, "but the king would be just one member, with only one vote when they decided things?"

"Right you are. Kings or rulers who had control over church business in their lands, whether they were Catholic or Protestant, did not want Calvin's way, because it would take away some of the ruler's power and give it to a gathering of preachers. They still don't. Are you ready for the next step toward Carolina?"

Of course, they wanted more of this unexpected story.

"Well, our John Knox ended up in Scotland," Elke continued, "where some of the big men had invited him. They had lots of power already, and they were trying to get more than the king or queen had. You see, there had not been a strong king or queen over Scotland for some while, so it was an easy time for the big men to push into the government. Most of them also wanted the Scottish church to change over to Calvin's ways. A lot of other people wanted that, too, mostly in the south and east, what they call the Lowland part of Scotland. That's the main trail of how the Church of Scotland became

Presbyterin, but it was not settled for good for more than a hundred years, either in Scotland or many of those lands on yon side of the 'Lantic Ocean."

Lizzy was wondering about something she didn't know how to ask. "Who got to decide whether to change the churches or not, and what to change them to?"

"Whoever had the government, or a big part of it, whether it was a little place or a big kingdom," Elke answered. "Lots of people moved, to be under a government that went for the kind of church they wanted. Folks either had to move, or change their ways of religion, or be punished for how they worshipped. My family said it was worst in the German places, because there are so many states there and no one government. The local rulers there fought one another already, and religion gave them one more thing to fight over. It was an unhappy time."

Elke stopped then and thought. "But think on this: mayhap some good came from it. More people paid attention to what their government was doing. Before, they mostly had not cared, because they had no say-so anyway. This showed up clearly in England and Scotland. Mixed in with what kind of church people wanted, there were questions about who should be on top in the government: should it be the king or the big men who were elected to make laws? In the air, too, was just what the rights of plain people were: how far could either the king or the lawmakers go in interfering with folk, like with taxes, or arrests, or saying what they could print in books and newspapers, or what churches they could have? These tangled-up questions kept coming up in the 1600s years. There were long meetings and battles about them. They got pretty well settled by about 1700. We are in the year 1764 now, so your grandparents likely heered about these happenings from their elders."

"Zounds," Ruly interrupted, all in a rush. "That must be summot what my Grandpa Morgin talked about. He was from Wells, or Wales, some country that was next to England, or maybe part of it, I dunno. Anyhow, they talked some language that was not English. I know he got his English after he moved to Car'liny. He's not long been dead. He used to go on a good deal about how Baptists and Quakers and Presbyterins and I don't know who-all had been mistreated in the old days. Why, they had to hide out just to have meetings, just to pray with more than four people outside their own houses! He had awful stories about them times, said his parents had been in it. Things got better, they said, after the big men who made the laws brought in 'King Billy.' I never knew if all that was so. Grandpa could make up a good yarn, and he claimed to be a Baptist hisself."

"That was no yarn. Many things that the English and Scots had been torn up over through the 1600s got settled then."

"Oh, I know what!" This time Lizzy was the excited one. "My mother told me about a "bill of rights" being written down over in England, making it plain what some of the rights of people are. Was that the times you are speaking of?"

"I think you girls have it fitting together about right, as far as I know."

More Questions for Elke

"Oh! What a sight of meat! Ye all are well into a night of work." Two Lincoln girls were carrying trenchers of bread, cheese, and steaming beer-pots of tea.

"What mercies you bring! Truly, we are obliged. Misses Lincoln, this is Elke Crying Bird. She came from Mrs. McBee's to nurse Mrs. Toliver's baby, and she is wonderful help to Ruly and me." The Lincolns made polite greetings and then turned back toward the tavern. Lizzy caught herself thinking the Lincolns were a trifle haughty.

Work halted while the three took their late supper. The skillets on the trivets needed more time to get hot enough to brown the meat quickly. While they ate, Molly joined them, with a small trencher and cup for herself. She had been standing a long time in the tavern and looked weary as well as sad. Lizzy sprang up from the seat that had been made from a stump, complete with a backrest. "Mrs. Molly, please sit here and enjoy your victuals. I thank you for your kindness with the hospitality."

Mrs. Strickland put her cup on the ground and sighed as she sat down. "You are welcome, Child, and I lament your grief."

"You have known Goody ever since she and Tomm moved here, I think, and you have lost a friend." Lizzy's voice was quiet.

"Even longer. We are cousins by marriage, though not by blood. I met Gudrun when she was a frisky little'un, same as me. My uncle had married her mother, a poor widow-woman, when we all lived in Virginia. Why, I saw her and Tomm marry. It was before I moved here with my husband. When she and Tomm came to this place, I'd not cast an eye on her since that day. You can imagine how we felt on realizing one another when they opened the public house right here on Middle Creek!"

They fell silent for a moment, but then Molly turned to Elke and asked, "No one has said exactly how she died. I heard she was all distracted-like and riding hard. Did the horse throw her? Did she go into labor during her ride? Did she die giving birth at McBee's? Please, Mrs. Crybird, if you were there when it happened, mayn't you put my mind to some ease?"

"The horse did not throw her, Ma'am, but she was dead or near about when they got to the place. The horse seemed to know where to go, straight to Gaspar's porch! Two o' the boys ran to fetch her down, but soon as that horse stopped, Mrs. Goody's body just slid on down from where she had balanced herself. I never would have imagined it! I saw them take her inside, and I ran to the chicken yard to get Minerva, hollering for Widow McBee."

"Did she ever know where she was or anything?"

"Not likely, Mrs. Molly, not likely. Never opened her eyes or said airy a word. Minerva and the widow worked with her for some time. It was said to me that they never felt her heart move or her chest rise. They said she had lost some body heat and it kept dropping, in spite of the covers. They all thought – we all thought – the baby was dead too, because it was blue and all misshapen when they pulled her out. Pulled her out – just like pulling out a calf, when the mamma can't push."

"Misshapen?"

"Yes'm. The little neck was all bent out, and its shoulders did not match up."

Molly shook her head. "From the hard riding, I'm a-thinking."

Ruly broke in with a frown: "Was Goody using a saddle?"

"No!" Elke almost smiled. "Mrs. McBee later opined that a saddle would have killed the baby! As it was, Mrs. Toliver managed to pull a leg over and ride sideways. She must have perched high and held her arms around the horse's neck as long as she could. That bent the baby's neck but did not break it or crush its little head. That it was a mercy."

Lizzy thought at least there was one thing good about Goody's wild flight: she forgot to saddle Snap. Lizzy wondered how much of the crisis the horse had sensed. Then, aloud, she asked:

"What all did Mrs. Minerva do to save the baby? Did you see any of that?"

"Ho! I more than saw it: I was part of it! She sent for me as soon as she took the baby into another room. When I got there, she had yarbs and powders next to the head and neck, and she kept warm cloths rubbing the baby all the time. I did not notice at first, but she had brought the afterbirth with the baby! She carried it in a bowl next to the baby, so the cord was still connected. I never knew such a thing. She was holding . . ."

Ruly's voice interrupted, like she was talking to herself. "Mayhap the afterbirth was still giving the baby what she needed for a while, before she – like – crossed over from the birthing?" Her eyes sought those of Molly, but the older woman only shook her head slowly, still focusing on Elke.

"Mrs. Minerva was holding the baby close," Elke went on. "As soon as I got there, she told me to remove my bodice and pull my shift down to my waist. I was puzzled, knowing the baby could not nurse, even if alive. I wanted to think the baby was breathing, but I could not feel it move. Mrs. Minerva told me to hold the baby as close to me as I could and be skin-to-skin with her and talk to her. *Talk* to her. What do you say to a dead or most-dead baby? I did not really think. I did pray out loud, and I sang a little. In German. It was just what I thought to do, being so scared. Mrs. Minerva slipped out and came back in with a clean piece of Mrs. Toliver's shift, which I guess smelled like her. Thinking back now, it may be that the baby could smell its way to life. Mayhap smelled my milk and its own mother! It seemed like a long time we kept this up. Mrs. Minerva said some words I did not understand, and some of her hope spread to me. We were begging the baby and the Lord at the same time, thinking how good it would be for her to live. When that little arm twitched and her mouth opened, we commenced to shouting and set everybody to running. All that night, I held the baby close, putting her down only to feed my Bentjamin. Mr. Tomm did not see the baby until after she was moving and crying and the cord had been cut, like a normal baby. Now her bent places are near about straightened out."

Molly smiled as she rose, touched Elke's arm, and went back into the tavern.

After Lizzy tested the heat of the skillets, she began placing the meat in them, and the other two joined her. They did not speak for a while. Goody's death and her baby's rise to life were mysteries to ponder and not speak. Then Lizzy asked the question she had been holding from before Molly had joined them. "Elke, how is it that you have come to know so much about the world beyond Carolina? You amazed us with your talk of Calvin and Europe and all."

"Way amazed," Ruly added. "I never expected to learn such things, even if I live four score years. And you're not much older'n me."

"My uncles were teachers and writers in Heidelberg, and they spent months at a time with us back in Pennsylvania. Their father, my grandfather, was a minister, educated at a university. He knew the sorrows and horrors of war. He spent his life leading people to think about why things were as they were. I may have told some things wrong this night, but I drew from family and neighbor talk. It is good that young women should understand such things.

Ruly had not finished her questions. She wanted to know about Ireland. "If the Presbyterins were the Church of Scotland, how come so many Presbyterins in these colonies are Irish?

Lizzy joined in. "It makes sense that families that came here from Scotland are Presbyterian, like Mrs. McBee. Mother told me that most people in Ireland are Catholic, and that the powerful people there, the ones who own most of the land, are Church of England people, not Catholic *or* Presbyterian. So why are so many Irish people over here Presbyterian?"

It was a hard question, but Elke answered it head-on.

"I heered it said that there are two kinds of Irish: the offspring of native stock and the offspring of move-ins. Most of the native, or "Old Irish," stayed Catholic during the religious changes, and they suffered from the wars as much as anybody, or more. Most of the move-in Irish are Scotch-Irish people. They have lived in Ireland for generations, too, but they moved in as Presbyterin and stayed that way. They are mostly in the north of Ireland, close by Scotland. The move-ins were farmers mostly, cheated of their land in Scotland and northern England or run off it during the wars. Some generals had taken over whole areas in the north of Ireland during Catholic rebellions in the 1600s. The generals sold the land to move-ins, but only to Protestants. This was during the time ordinary people were moving around in most of Europe, trying to match their religion with the government, as well find ways to make a living after their homes, farms, and whole towns had been destroyed."

"So most Irish in Ireland are Catholic, but there are fewer Catholics in the north of Ireland and more Scotch-Irish move-ins there? And the Scotch-Irish are mostly Presbyterian farmers?" Lizzy tried to hold on to what she understood as she turned the meat in the skillets, using long forked sticks.

Ruly followed, asking, "And a lot of Scotch-Irish must have moved from the north of Ireland to Ameriky and are still coming?"

"You're both right. Here in the Carolinas and Virginia, the Irish are Scotch-Irish, but they just call themselves Irish. In some other colonies, there are both kinds of Irish people."

The coals were mighty hot. The three did not talk as they browned the meat pieces quickly and placed them in the big pot over the low fire. The water had come to a boil, but Lizzy knew not to let it boil with the meat in it. She wanted especially good food for Goody's burying day. It would comfort Tomm, she knew, and Goody's cooking deserved a tribute. The stew would simmer all night, and toward morning, the piles of prepared vegetables would be added. Lizzy intended to spend the night near the pot so she could stir it with the wash paddle to keep it from sticking or lumping. Flour was the secret for a smooth thick stew, but it needed watching.

As they moved the skillets away from the fire and waited for them to cool enough to handle, Elke spoke. "Now I will go in to the babies. I feed little Sunilda every two or three hours, and my breasts are paining me. It is a blessing to have milk enough for two! Ruly and I will take turns with the stew. You must sleep, Lizzy, for you have many cares and duties tomorrow."

As Elke turned, Ruly declared, "Your grandpap would be right proud of you this night. We value your help to understand how things are in North Car'liny right now. You have cleared up in my mind some matters that had not made sense before, and they troubled me." Lizzy could not agree more.

Safe in Their Nests

The next night, when Lizzy dropped onto her straw, she thought through the burial day that finally was over. Mostly, she felt relieved. Tomm had carried his sorrow with dignity. Dear Mr. Marshall had looked after things and spoke the burial. It was not a long talk, but his words fit Goody when she had been at her best. The people sang over the grave and dropped flowers on the casket. The grave was up the hill a-ways, in Goody's orchard. The air was sweet with ripening pears Lizzy would gather soon.

Feeding people this day, like the night before, had been in Lizzy's hands. She knew she had done well, and she was thankful it was plenty and extra-good. All the people who helped her: "Lord bless them," she breathed.

She had stayed on her feet with the food and all, but her tiredness was mixed with two joys that had come to her this sad day. She ran them through her mind again to relive the pleasure.

First, Squire Needham and his lady had arrived early, and who had they brought with them but her own Davo?! After she and Davo hugged, the squire told them they would have some time to visit after most of the company had gone, and he sent Davo to the stable to handle visitors' horses, like Wa'ro had done.

After the burial and the eating, Lizzy took food for herself and Davo to the stable yard. They had a right good chinwag, halting when anyone needed his horse for leaving. Davo wanted the details on how she had got him away from Leetch and who-all had helped. He had her tell it over and over, couldn't get enough. Lizzy told him a lot about Ruly and her way with horses, and about the Morgins and Lincolns, and about Zeke and the women bringing the vittles for a stew. That was after Davo declared it the best stew of his life.

Lizzy could tell he was getting plenty to eat, but she asked anyway about how the Needhams treated him. He went quiet and started to cry but spoke up strongly, "Liz, she is more like our mother than I would ever think. I do all the jobs for her I can, and she never chides me, and she tells me I have good in me. After all the torment at that devil Leetch's, I thought I was ruint and could never be my good self no more. I don't spend most of my time at their place now. Squire has loaned me out to a powerful good mechanic. I am learning how to make looms and fix them when they break. I never thought about looms breaking so much. Mayhap weavers get careless. But that is my special talent."

Davo was excited now, and it filled Lizzy's heart to see it. "Fixing broke looms! I do near 'bout all of the repair jobs that come in. Did you know there's different ways to build looms? They're not all the same, no never. And when one comes in like

I've not seen afore, I get to take it apart and see how it was first set up to work."

"You like the work, then. Squire Needham did a good thing putting you in the way of a useful trade." With some reluctance, she asked, "Is he teaching you to read and write, or do you think he really will? Seems like you and the squire both might be too busy for that."

"He has started me his own self. I had forgot much of what Mother taught me, but he fills that in on the Sabbath and other times when I stay at their house. He gave me some things to copy during the week a few times, but there is not enough paper for copying. I will skin off some bark when the birches dry out this winter."

Lizzy knew what she could do about the papers, but she hoped copying would not be the extent of the Mr. Needham's educating Little Brother.

"He says I am a fast learner," the boy went on. "He even has said he will do his best to get me under a proper schoolteacher, one that comes through here. I heered the missus urge him to do that, Liz, when they did not know I was about."

Davo looked away a moment, like he was deciding to say more. His tear wells filled again, and he whispered, "Liz, she told him I was the nearest to a son they ever would have, and that I was deserving in my own right. I had the feeling that Mother had sent me two angels. I value them above all I know, except you, Liz, and they are up there alongside you in my mind. I value thinking he could be like our own poor Papa to me. I vow to never betray Squire Needham's trust."

Lizzy could hardly believe such heartfelt words came from a boy not yet ten. Mother had raised him gently, but this talk was beyond her imagining. Maybe it had something to do with bad treatment by the wagon maker and natural gratitude. So she ventured,

"Little brother, I could see you were mistreated at Leetch's. Can you tell me what it was like?"

He pulled back and showed her a face she had never seen before.

"No, damn you to hell, I will NOT speak of it, EVER! It is gone, it is NOT ME or any part of me."

The corners of Davo's mouth were filled with spit! She had never seen this. It was not her Davo. How she wished she could take the question back from his hearing! She could not think what to say and tried to think of Mother.

"I will not trouble you about it again. We will think on all that is good, your new home and training – and that the good squire will let us see one another. That's what matters."

On her straw bed, Lizzy kept thinking about Davo. Most of their visit told her he was happier than she knew, like a new-flying bird glorifying the air. The other part was so unlike him. How could they be the same person?

She moved from her mixed thoughts to the perfect bliss that took her to sleep. It had come from Minerva. She had arrived with the widow a short time before the burial, both of them well-dressed and with a manner of respect toward Tomm that did not suggest their own importance. Minerva helped serve food easily, not making any fuss. After she had been around Lizzy a while, she stood next to her, looking at the floor but easy in her stance. "I'm sorry we couldn't save Miz Goody. She was too broke up when they fetched her into the house."

"But you saved the baby she was trying so hard to have! Thank you!"

Minerva's eyes met Lizzy's gaze to receive the thanks. Then they looked beyond Lizzy, not down. No one but Lizzy could see or hear what Minerva said next.

"You will want to know that the birds you helped to fly are safe in their nest."

Lizzy's legs went limp. She nearly dropped to the floor as Minerva walked away.

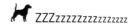 ZZZzzzzzzzzzzzzzzzz

Dedication

to
Mary Grace,
a daughter of Old Johnston County,
who already shares some of Lizzy's wisdom and common
sense.

Acknowledgements

The Red Dog benefits from George Troxler's good
nature, his historian's insights, and his work with the
cover photograph.
Thanks also to Deborah Beckel for reading the
manuscript and asking good questions
and to Wayne Drumheller for generous advice and
encouragement.

About the Author and this Book

Carole Troxler interrupted her work with the Revolutionary Era to write this book, her only fiction piece. Capable of curmudgeonly conduct, she began writing *The Red Dog* to entertain herself at the beach while her husband, whom she adores, was adoring the Atlantic Ocean and she was not. The book became an obsession, a common occurrence. Carole loves living in the woods along Travis Creek in Alamance County. She encourages native plants there and sometimes plays Old-Time Music with very special people. Carole and George Troxler are in their fiftieth year of marriage. They are blessed with two accomplished and happy daughters, the world's cutest grandbaby, a near-grand-daughter whose elegance inspired Lizzy's manner, and outstanding in-laws all around.

A native of LaGrange, Georgia, she has received two book awards and the North Carolina Literary and Historical Association's Christopher Crittenden Award.

Non-fiction books by Carole Watterson Troxler

- *The Loyalist Experience in North Carolina* (1976)
- *Shuttle & Plow: A History of Alamance County, North Carolina* (co-author with William Murray Vincent, 1999)
- *Pyle's Defeat: Deception at the Race Path* (2003)
- *Alamance County, North Carolina, Transcripts of Census and Tax Records* (2003)
- *Farming Dissenters: The Regulator Movement in Piedmont North Carolina* (2011)
- *Sallie Stockard and the Adversities of an Educated Woman of the New South* (scheduled for publication, 2018)

Made in the USA
Columbia, SC
20 January 2018